Epic Myths
for Fearless
Girls

Retold by
**Claudia
Martin**

Illustrated by
Khoa Le

ARCTURUS

ARCTURUS

This edition published in 2023 by Arcturus Publishing Limited
26/27 Bickels Yard, 151–153 Bermondsey Street,
London SE1 3HA

Author: Claudia Martin
Illustrator: Khoa Le
Editor: Donna Gregory
Designer: Allie Oldfield
Design Manager: Jessica Holliland

ISBN: 978-1-3988-1124-9
CH010055NT
Supplier 29, Date 1122, PI 00003001

Printed in China

Contents

Introduction

From Sedna of the Arctic to Isis of Egypt, the mighty goddesses and daring girls in these myths battle demons, outwit giants, and save the world from disaster. When everyone else runs away in fear, these girls face up to the scariest of monsters and live to tell the tale.

Even though these girls are daring, they do not always feel brave. Sometimes, they are frightened. Sometimes, they doubt they are strong enough for their task. Sometimes, they cry because they feel alone and hopeless. Yet when they grit their teeth and take a deep breath, they all dare to stand up for what is right.

For some of our heroines, such as Durga the ten-armed warrior, being daring means wielding a sword with a strong hand and heart. Yet, for others, being daring means only believing in yourself when no one else does. This is what Oochigeas manages in a myth told by the Mi'kmaq, a First Nations people of Canada. Without weapons or even shoes, she dares to stand up for herself. In a Yoruba myth from West Africa, the smallest of the gods and goddesses, Oshun, dares to stop doubting herself.

For quite a few of our heroines, being daring means admitting they are wrong, which can be the hardest feat of all. When the Polynesian goddess Hina realizes she has failed in her task, she admits she made a mistake—only after facing up to her failure, can she dust herself off and try again.

Myths were told long before there were books and even before there was writing. Myths were spoken or sung around the evening fire, or whispered to children as they drifted off to sleep. Myths were exciting stories that made their listeners gasp or laugh. Myths were also a way of explaining how the world came to be as it is.

Many of our myths try to explain the beauty we see around us, from blooming plants and sparkling stars to golden sunsets, and they can also try to explain why there are things that can hurt us—storms, droughts, wildfires, floods. Ancient storytellers needed to talk about why there is both good and bad in our world. This is why many of our goddesses can also be both good and bad. While they can water the fields or quench fires, they can also make violent volcanoes or hide the Sun itself, bringing terrifying darkness.

Like the people who first told myths long ago, and like all of us today, our goddesses and heroines have their faults. The Japanese Sun goddess Amaterasu is a little too proud of her beauty. The Hawai'ian goddess Pele has a terrible temper. Over the centuries, some tellers of the Ancient Greek story of Pandora have blamed everything that is wrong in the world, from sickness to war, on Pandora's faults. They told us that if Pandora had not been disobedient, we would all be perfectly happy, all the time. When you read Pandora's story, you can decide for yourself what you think about this!

Eventually, perhaps hundreds of years after these myths were first told, they were written down for the first time. The earliest writers, and every writer after them, put their own twist on the old myths, mixing in their own experiences, hopes, and fears. When you read the story of Oochigeas, you may notice similarities to the well-known fairy tale Cinderella. It is possible that our version of Oochigeas's story was influenced by Cinderella, probably the version of the famous tale written by Charles Perrault in 1697. Our unknown Mi'kmaq storyteller picked out the ideas they liked and threw out the rest, including the fairy godmother.

In this book, we have dared to tweak the endings to two of the European myths. In the best-known stories about Scandinavia's Freyja and Ireland's Étaín, the goddesses stay at home while the boys feast with giants or test their skill at the game of Fidchell. We will never know if the original myths were changed over the centuries, perhaps by writers who did not think girls should have too much fun. But no daring girl wants to read about girls who stay at home while the boys have all the fun! In our stories, Étaín and Freyja set out on their own daring adventures. They make their own decisions. They can write the stories of their own lives.

And so can you. Take a deep breath and dare ...

How Japlo Stole Mami Wata's Comb

Based on Liberian myths

A long time ago, on the sandy, sun-soaked shores of Liberia lived a young girl named Japlo. She lived with her little brother, Nyennoh, and their father. They were very happy, but they were not rich. As long as Japlo's father was able to go to sea each day, he was able to catch enough to keep them all fed and well.

One night, a terrible storm blew in from the ocean. Japlo hugged Nyennoh tightly as the winds howled outside their house. In the morning, when the storm had blown itself out, the two of them hurried down to the beach to see the damage. Japlo gasped when she saw her father's boat halfway up the beach. There was a jagged hole in the boat's side, large enough to crawl inside, and the fishing nets were torn.

"What will Father do now, Japlo?" asked Nyennoh, tugging on her hand. "He'll still be able to go fishing, won't he?" Japlo wanted to tell Nyennoh that everything would be fine, but she knew Father would never be able to mend a hole that big. And without the boat there would be no fish. Their bowls would be empty.

But she couldn't bear to worry Nyennoh. "It'll be alright," she choked out. Her throat was sore from holding back tears.

Farther along the beach, in the shade of the palms, people were sitting in a circle on the sand. "Let's go see what's happening," said Nyennoh, scampering away. "It looks like a storyteller!" he yelled over his shoulder.

Japlo raced after her brother, her feet kicking up plumes of sand.

The storyteller was holding a kora between his knees, plucking its strings with quick, clever fingers. He was singing a story that Japlo had heard before about a water spirit.

"And Mami Wata gave our hero all he asked for,
She begged him to return her precious comb,
But our hero held tight the stolen comb,
So Mami Wata gave our hero all he asked for ..."

The audience sang along with the storyteller's chorus, clapping and gasping at the right moments. As Japlo listened, she wished that life was as simple as the story. If she could really find Mami Wata and steal her precious comb, she could ask the water spirit for all she wanted. And all she wanted was a new boat for Father.

When the storyteller was packing up, Japlo sidled over. "I enjoyed your story," she said politely. "If ... someone ... wanted to find Mami Wata, where should they go?"

The storyteller looked at Japlo sharply. "Go right down to the edge of the water, just as the sun is setting at the end of the day," he said slowly. "But beware of greedy water spirits, child. Be careful taking anything Mami Wata offers. Whatever she gives, she takes something in return."

But Japlo and Nyennoh were already racing home across the beach. Japlo did not hear the storyteller's warning. Or perhaps she did not want to hear.

That evening, as the sun was painting the sky pink and purple, Japlo walked down to the beach alone. And there, just as the storyteller promised, was Mami Wata. It was almost too simple. Japlo gulped.

The water spirit was sitting on a rock a little way out from the shore. The waves splashed and frothed around the rock, and the scales of her golden tail glittered in the

sunlight. Water snakes writhed around her shoulders, their tongues darting. And all the while, Mami Wata combed her hair with her ornate comb.

Japlo knew what she must do. She needed to distract Mami Wata so she could steal her comb. Her heart pounded as she picked up a coconut from the warm sand. She crept closer to the spirit, ducking behind a rock whenever Mami Wata glanced in her direction.

When Japlo felt she was near enough, she hurled the coconut as hard as she could. It plopped into the water behind Mami Wata. Startled, the spirit gazed around her. Then, with one swift wriggle of her tail, Mami Wata dived into the water to find which mackerel or snapper had disturbed her. She left her precious comb lying on the rock.

There was not a moment to lose. Japlo waded into the water, gasping as the waves broke at her waist, her chest, her chin. She clambered onto the slippery rock, seized the comb, and sloshed back to the beach. Now Mami Wata hauled herself out of the water onto her empty rock.

Mami Wata saw Japlo right away. Her eyes burned with fury. Her snakes hissed. "Ssssssso, little girl," she spat, "you've sssssssstolen my comb."

"I'm so sorry, it's just that my father's boat is wrecked and he needs a new one so much and I hoped that you might give us a new one," gabbled Japlo.

"Ssssssince you have my comb," said Mami Wata, "I must give you all you ask for. I will sssssee you when I need sssssssomething in return."

And with a splash, Mami Wata was gone.

Japlo looked at the comb in her hands. It was heavier than she had expected. Its teeth were sharper. She hid it in the folds of her dress and hurried home to bed.

Soon after sunrise, she awoke to the sound of her father shouting excitedly. "You won't believe it!" he yelled. "Someone has mended my boat. It's as good as new!"

Japlo's little family cried tears of joy. Nyennoh leaped up and down, yelping with delight. Japlo thought of the sharp teeth of Mami Wata's comb.

When no one was looking, Japlo ran down to the water's edge and placed Mami Wata's comb on her rock. She hoped, she hoped with all her heart, that the comb would satisfy Mami Wata. Just in case the spirit was still angry, Japlo decided to stay away from

the beach. In fact, she would stay away from all water, from every stream, every pond, so Mami Wata would not be able to find her.

When Father came home that evening, his basket was filled to the brim with fish. Nyennoh and Japlo set to work with a frying pan, baobab leaves, and alligator pepper. "Can you fetch some more firewood, Japlo?" asked Father.

Japlo went out to the wood pile and stretched up high to reach the driest logs. Something slithered around her ankle. She froze. A snake was coiling itself around her leg. It was slithering higher, its scales slipping across her skin.

"Ssssso," said the snake. "Here I am."

"Oh, Mami Wata," gasped Japlo. The logs fell from her shaking hands.

"Sssssince you took the thing I love the mosssst, in return I will take what you love the mosssst."

"B-But I gave you back your comb," stammered Japlo, sinking to her knees.

"Sssssilly girl," hissed Mami Wata. "That'sss not the bargain we ssstruck. Let me ssssee." She wriggled, her scales glittering. "You love little Nyennoh the mossssssst, sssso I will take him to live with me beneath the sssssssea."

"No!" shouted Japlo. "You can't have him! You can't have Ny-Ny. You can't! You can have me instead. Take me instead, please."

Mami Wata's tongue flickered as if tasting the air. "Ssssee you," she said, uncoiling herself from Japlo's leg and slithering away into the darkness.

Japlo ran inside and hugged Ny-Ny tight. And she hugged him all that night as he slept beside her, and every night after that. As the nights passed, Japlo began to hope

that Mami Wata had forgotten about their bargain. Months went by, until Japlo told herself that Ny-Ny was safe, that Mami Wata would not take him away.

One morning, Father asked Nyennoh and Japlo to help him cast the nets from his boat. As Father paddled out into the bay, Japlo held Ny-Ny safe on her lap. They watched the village become no more than a streak on the horizon.

Japlo felt Nyennoh shivering. She looked up at the sun, but it was hidden behind dark, rushing clouds. Now she saw that the waves had started to foam and crest.

"Storm coming," yelled Father over the rising wind.

The waves were growing taller and stronger, tossing the boat up and down. Water poured over the sides. They held each other tight. Nyennoh started to cry. The waves swung them up and down, up and—over! The water surged up to meet them.

Water filled Japlo's eyes, her mouth, her nose. Her arms were empty. Where was Ny-Ny? Where was Father? She thrashed and kicked in panic, seeing nothing but water. Then she saw Ny-Ny deep below her, his arms and legs waving. Japlo pulled fiercely through the water, reaching for him. But she was not fast enough. There was Mami Wata, powering through the water with flicks of her shimmering tail.

Mami Wata grabbed Ny-Ny's arm. Japlo grasped Mami Wata's hand.

"Take me, please, not him," Japlo shouted into the water.

Mami Wata shook her head. Wriggling her tail, Mami Wata pulled them along behind her until Japlo's strength was gone, her breath was gone.

Mami Wata realized that Japlo had been selfless—she had only asked for help that had been desperately needed and had been prepared to pay the cost of her request with her own life. She headed back to the boat with the two children in tow.

Japlo's head broke the surface of the ocean. She gasped air into her burning chest.

Mama Wata whispered in Japlo's ear: "You're a good ssssister."

With a shove, Mami Wata tumbled Japlo and Ny-Ny over the side of the boat. A moment later, she pushed Father in to join them. Then she was gone.

The three of them lay at the bottom of the boat, holding each other's hands. When the sun came out, Father paddled toward the shore. Japlo watched the waves for Mami Wata's beautiful face, but she never saw her, not ever again.

Freyja's Necklace

Based on Norse myths

Many moons ago, the old Norse gods walked the Earth. Some of the Norse people who revered them were peaceful farmers, but others were Viking warriors. The Vikings were known throughout the world for their fearless spirit and courage in battle.

They sailed far and wide, and would fight any enemies they found. At the end of the day, those who were still alive would go to the nearest hall, where they would feast together and toast their victory.

The reason the Vikings were not afraid was because if they died in battle, they knew that a fine reward waited for them. Half of the dead would be picked by the god Odin to go to his great hall, called Valhalla. The other half would be taken by the goddess Freyja to her hall, Sessrúmnir. In those halls, the warriors would feast and fight happily forever.

Freyja was the most important of all the goddesses, and she was ready to get married. Giant after giant came to ask to marry her. There was the king of the giants himself, Thrymr, as well as noisy Hrungnir, and Fjolverkr the builder. She refused them all.

Freyja always wore a necklace, named Brísingamen, made of finely worked gold. She loved Brísingamen above all objects, not because it was gold, but because she had won it in battle. Freyja also wore a cloak of rustling falcon feathers. This magical cloak gave Freyja the gift of flight.

One evening, as Freyja's warriors were served with goblets of mead and trays of sausages, she saw the god Loki slide into the hall. Freyja knew that wherever Loki went, trouble followed close behind. He could change his shape as fast as he changed his friends.

Freyja sighed. She waved Loki forward. "Loki, what brings you to Sessrúmnir?"

"Most beautiful goddess," crooned Loki, his sharp eyes flicking left and right. "I come with terrible news."

It was just as Freyja had expected. "What is it?" she asked grimly.

The boar Hildisvíni trotted to Freyja's side. His tusks were sharp and his hair was bristly, but he was Freyja's most trusted friend.

Loki clasped a hand to his chest as if trying to still his pounding heart. "This morning," he whispered loudly, "the great god Thor woke to find his magic hammer, Mjölnir, had been stolen. We soon received a message from Thrymr, king of the giants. If we do not give Thrymr what he wants, he will use Mjölnir to take power."

Freyja gasped. Every blow from Mjölnir brought thunder, storms, and destruction. If Thrymr had the hammer, there would be chaos.

"So what does Thrymr want?" asked Hildisvíni gruffly.

"I'm glad you asked," said Loki. "Thrymr wants to marry the most beautiful goddess of them all." With a flourish, he bowed toward Freyja. "So, if you will come with me, my lovely Freyja, we will deliver you to Thrymr and get this sorted out in no time."

Freyja felt the prickling of anger. "Deliver me?" she said, trying to keep her voice steady. "Like a sack of hay?"

Loki's eyes flickered over Freyja's flushed face. "I know you wouldn't want Mjölnir to stay in the wrong hands," he said slyly.

Freyja looked down at Hildisvíni. "What do you think, Hildisvíni, should I do as I'm told? Or—" Her voice rose to a shout, silencing the singing warriors the length and

breadth of the hall, "should I let these gods sort out their own problems? Get out, Loki, and don't come back." She pointed at the door.

Bowing low, Loki backed out of the hall. But where Loki could not find a direct route to his goal, he would find a twisting one. He knew Freyja loved her necklace. If he could steal Brísingamen, Freyja would do whatever she was told in order to get it back.

That night, when Freyja lay sleeping in her bedroom, Loki transformed himself into a bulging-eyed fly. His wings buzzing, he flew to Freyja's door and squeezed through the keyhole. He landed on Freyja's cheek and gleefully rubbed together his hairy legs. But Freyja's left hand was resting on Brísingamen. In a blink of an eye, the trickster changed himself into a flea and bit poor Freyja's skin. Deep in her dreams, the goddess lifted her hand to brush away the pest.

Now Loki transformed himself back into a god, snatched Brísingamen, and snuck out. He sniggered to himself as he scampered away into the night.

When Freyja woke in the dawn, she felt at once that her neck was bare. She knew that no one other than Loki could be the culprit. Freyja threw on her cloak of falcon feathers and called for her chariot.

The goddess's chariot was not pulled by tall horses or fierce wolves but by two small and furry cats. Seeing their mistress so upset, the little cats stopped playing with their ball of yarn and slipped into their harnesses. With Hildisvíni galloping alongside, the cats pulled Freyja over the mountains, straight to the fort of Thrúdheim, the home of Thor.

Freyja pounded on the oak door. "Thor! Let me in this instant!"

The door to the great hall swung open. There stood Thor, his massive legs planted like tree trunks. His eyebrows bristled like caterpillars. His bushy red beard looked ready for nesting birds. Beside Thor was grinning Loki, twirling Brísingamen between his fingers.

Thor was known for his terrible temper, but Freyja was too angry to think twice. "Give me back what is mine," she ordered.

"You'll get your necklace back," cackled Loki. "As soon as Thrymr has his bride."

Freyja ignored Loki. "Thor, you won't get my help by stealing from me. If you want Thrymr to have a bride, marry him yourself!"

To Freyja's surprise, Thor began to laugh. His guffaws shook the rafters of the hall. "I'm not sure that I'm his type," he said when he stopped laughing.

"Well, we don't always get what we want," said Freyja with a toss of her head. Then she fell silent, an idea growing in her mind. "Mmmm," she said at last. "If you do exactly as I say, Thor, I'll get you back Mjölnir and give Thrymr the surprise of his life."

"How?" boomed Thor eagerly.

"Loki," ordered Freyja, "go and tell Thrymr that I am eager to marry him. Tell him to prepare a wedding feast and invite all the giants. My handmaiden and I will arrive this evening to celebrate our glorious marriage. And, Loki," she said firmly, "you must leave Brísingamen here with me."

Sensing a plan to rival one of his own, Loki did exactly as he was told.

Right away, Freyja sent Hildisvíni to fetch a wedding dress, the largest he could find. Then she picked the prettiest flowers from the meadow. She chose purple harebells and pink meadowrue, sweet-scented orchid, and delicate willowherb.

"Now," said Freyja to Thor, "you must put on this lovely dress."

"What?" bellowed Thor furiously.

Freyja tugged the wedding dress over Thor's bulging shoulders.

"I don't think I'm exactly what Thrymr had in mind for a bride," yelled Thor, thrashing with his broad fists.

She raised a finger in warning. "This is the only way to teach him that he can't order a bride like he's ordering his dinner," she said firmly.

"And that he can't steal from the gods," muttered Thor.

While Thor stood patiently, Freyja decorated his beard with a pink ribbon and dressed his unruly hair with flowers. She stood back to admire the result, but it was still obvious that the bride was a battle-scarred old god, not a beautiful young goddess.

Thinking quickly, Freyja ripped a piece of cloth from her petticoat and put it over Thor's face as a veil. Finally, she fastened Brísingamen round Thor's neck.

Then Freyja and Thor raced to Jotunheim, land of the giants. Thrymr greeted them at the door of his hall. "Welcome, welcome," he roared. The giant was taller even than Thor, and nearly as broad as he was high.

"Here is the beautiful Freyja," said Freyja, pulling the veiled Thor forward.

"She's taller than I thought she would be!" said Thrymr. "I see you're wearing your famous Brísingamen, as always," he bellowed in Thor's face. "Please, come and enjoy the delicious feast I have prepared for you."

With a thump that almost broke the bench, Thor sat down next to Thrymr. Freyja sat on Thrymr's other side. The assembled giants took their seats. Never one to turn down delicious food, Thor fell on the feast greedily. He ate a whole side of beef, sixteen sausages, and four loaves of bread. He swilled it all down with a barrel of mead, and then burped loudly.

"Goodness me," said Thrymr, nervously, to Freyja. "My bride has a hearty appetite."

"Poor Freyja has been so excited about meeting you that she has not eaten in eight days," said Freyja quickly.

"Well," roared Thrymr, rubbing his hands together, "then I shall give her a kiss."

Leaning forward to plant a kiss on his bride, the giant caught sight of Thor's eyes glaring furiously through his thin veil. "She has very piercing eyes," gasped Thrymr.

"Freyja has been so longing for her wedding that she has not been able to sleep for eight nights," gabbled Freyja.

"Wonderful," said Thrymr, rising to his feet, "let's get on with the wedding then."

"Wait," said Freyja, putting a hand on the giant's arm. "Now you have your bride, you must give me Thor's hammer, Mjölnir."

"With pleasure," said Thrymr graciously, waving forward a burly giant. The fierce fellow put heavy Mjölnir in Freyja's hands.

With a flourish, Thor ripped his veil off to reveal his face to Thrymr.

Thrymr bellowed in outrage. "You are not young and beautiful," he shouted, "but old and hairy, with a face like a blind smith's thumb!"

"How dare you!" roared Thor, angered by the insult. "That is very rude—and what do you expect? You can't just demand a wife in return for a stolen hammer!" He swung his thick arm round Thrymr's neck, ready to make him sorry he had ever tried to trick the gods.

Holding Mjölnir tightly, Freyja flew into the air, her cloak of falcon feathers whistling behind her. As she swooped through the door, she turned back to see Thor and Thrymr kicking over tables and flailing their arms. All the giants were roaring with laughter as the pair continued to trade blows and insults. Freyja allowed herself a sly smile. Not only had she retrieved the hammer, she had also taught Thor and Thrymr a valuable lesson—they would never try to trade a goddess for anything ever again!

Durga and the
Buffalo Demon

Based on Indian myths

Long, long ago, the gods ruled over the land of India. They sat in the heavens and watched over Earth, taking care of the people who lived below. There was also a kingdom of demons. The demons were always at war with the gods, trying to destroy them, but the gods had powerful weapons and always beat the demons.

One day, a new prince of the demons was born. He was part demon and part buffalo. His name was Mahishasura and he could shapeshift into anything he wanted. The king of the demons was thrilled—his son would finally be able to defeat the gods.

As Mahishasura grew older and cleverer, he came up with a cunning plan to defeat the gods once and for all. For a full year Mahishasura sat under a tree and prayed to the god Brahma, creator of all things. Impressed by Mahishasura's devotion, Brahma offered to give him a reward to encourage him to stay on the side of the gods.

"Oh, there's just one small thing I desire, my lord," said Mahishasura sneakily. "Let no god, man, or animal have the power to kill me."

Brahma granted the demon's wish. But now there was nothing to stop Mahishasura

from terrorizing both humans and gods. The wicked buffalo leaped through the heavens, destroying the city of the gods with his hooves.

Mahishasura believed he was lord of all. His flesh could not be pierced by the gods' weapons. Mahishasura trampled crops under his horned feet. He kicked up storms. He head-butted mountains. The gods gazed down at the frightened, huddled humans and knew that something must be done.

Ten of the gods gathered in the Himalayas, among the clouds that cloaked the world's tallest mountains.

"How can we rid the world of this demon?" cried Surya, god of the Sun. "No god, no man, no animal can hurt him!"

Now Brahma, the all-knowing god, spoke: "All is not lost. In all Mahishasura's arrogance, it never entered his head that he might be defeated by a woman."

Vishnu, god of protection, managed a smile. "But we will need a goddess so strong, so wise, so good,

that Mahishasura will run in terror. We will have to make her."

"That would take all our strength ..." murmured Ganesh, god of luck. He scratched his long, elephant's trunk. "Can we even do it?"

"We must try," answered Varuna, god of the sea.

And so the gods joined hands and, with all of their energy, all of their power, they tried to will a goddess into existence. At first, nothing happened. Then, at the heart of the circle, a faint light flickered. The light burned brighter until it blazed hotter than the Sun. Blinded, the gods pressed their hands to their eyes. When they could bear to squint into the light, there she was—a goddess who looked a lot like a human girl.

She was smaller than they had hoped. She did not look very strong. But there was a fierceness to her gaze that made the gods keep their thoughts to themselves. The girl had ten arms, one for each of the gods who had made her.

"We must give her weapons," said Shiva, god of destruction. He stepped forward, his serpent writing around his neck. "Take my trident," he said to the new goddess. She took the trident with her first hand.

Next came Brahma, whose four heads saw all. He placed a perfect lotus flower in the goddess's second hand. "This flower brings great wisdom, without which all battles are lost."

The third god to step forward was Vishnu, holding his round, sharp-edged discus. "This weapon will destroy evil if it is thrown with a pure heart." The goddess nodded, taking the discus in her third hand.

The fourth god was Yama, god of death, who gave her his sword. He was followed by Vayu and Surya, gods of the wind and sun, who gave her a bow and an arrow. The seventh god was Tvashtr, the maker god, with his mace, which he often used to strike heavy blows against tricksters. Ganesh handed the goddess a rope looped into a noose, and Indra, god of the sky, offered his vajra, a special weapon to unleash thunderbolts.

Last came Varuna, god of the sea. He placed his conch shell in the goddess's tenth hand. "Blow into this shell with all your strength, and its terrible sound will lay waste to armies."

"You are ready to seek Mahishasura," said Brahma to the figure in front of him, "but first you need a name. I call you Durga, which means undefeatable."

Durga was about to clamber down the mountain when Himavat, lord of the Himalayas, scrambled breathlessly up the slope, his white beard whipping behind him. "Wait! You can't go into battle on foot! You must ride my lion."

With a fearful roar, a lion sprang onto the mountaintop. The gods gasped. But Durga was not afraid. She reached out a hand to stroke the lion's wild mane. The fierce creature kneeled at Durga's feet so she could climb on its back.

Now Durga galloped away on her lion. When she reached the plain where Mahishasura had set up camp with his army, Durga called to a demon soldier: "Go and tell Mahishasura that I demand his surrender. If he will not agree to live in peace, I will slay him. Tell him to come and give me his answer."

When the buffalo demon heard that a girl was demanding his surrender, he laughed

so hard that his sides hurt. He knew exactly how to trick a girl. At once, he transformed himself into a handsome man. Only his horns and hooves remained.

Mahishasura swaggered over to where Durga waited, her hands on her weapons.

"I was told a beautiful goddess had arrived," said Mahishasura, "but nothing could have prepared me for your loveliness. I cannot stop the blushes from spreading across my cheeks. I confess I have fallen head over heels in love with you!"

Durga raised an eyebrow. "I suggest you take your situation more seriously. Will you surrender to me?"

Mahishasura clasped his hand to his heart. "If you will only agree to marry me, I will do anything you ask of me."

Durga had not been expecting this at all. She started to giggle. "You think I'll be fooled by your tricks?" she managed to choke out. Her laughter grew into a rumble of thunder that shook the ground and sent snow sliding down the mountainsides.

The silly smile fell from Mahishasura's face. Now he began to see the danger he was in. At once, he transformed himself into a buffalo. Mahishasura's demon soldiers raced toward Durga. But, quick as lightning, she blew into her conch shell. Deafened, the demons pressed their hands to their ears but—as she blew and blew—they crumbled into dust.

All that day, Mahishasura and Durga battled, but she could not land a blow on his hairy hide. On the second day, he transformed into a tiger that slashed and bit with claws and teeth. Durga shook her vajra, sending a thunderbolt that hurtled Mahishasura to the ground. But the tiger sprang back on its feet. On the third day, Mahishasura became an elephant. Durga twirled her rope, looping its noose around the elephant's trunk. She yanked the demon off his feet, but at once he became a snake and slithered away.

The battle went on for nine long and exhausting days. As the demon shifted into the shape of an eagle, leopard, bear, wolf, crocodile, and scorpion, Durga struggled to strike him with her weapons. Her arrow fell short, her sword missed its mark, and her discus only skimmed his ear.

Exhausted and thirsty, Durga began to despair. Mahishasura sensed her weakness and taunted her, saying, "You will never defeat me. You see, you are only a woman. I am anything I want to be!" She felt hopeless. All the gods, all the world's people, were relying on her to defeat this demon. She feared she would let them down. She wanted to run away and hide, where no one could see her shame. But she fought on.

On the tenth day, Durga jabbed her trident while Mahishasura turned back into a buffalo. To her surprise, the trident grazed the buffalo's shoulder. Mahishasura roared with anger. He began to change shape, first his head and then his arms taking human form. Durga saw her chance—caught between forms, the demon was at his weakest. She thrust hard with her trident—and pricked the demon's leg. Mahishasura fell onto his back, his hooves kicking the air. Summoning the last of her strength, Durga plunged the trident into the buffalo demon's belly. And with a bellow of rage, the demon was dead.

Durga wiped the dust and tears from her eyes. She stroked her loyal lion. Then she made her way to the city of the gods, where she would wait until she was needed again.

Amaterasu
and the Cave

Based on Japanese myths

In the early days of the world, the islands of Japan did not yet exist. The creator god, Izanami, and her husband, Izanagi, looked down on the churning seas and decided to make new land. Izanami dipped her glittering spear into the ocean and stirred.

"Look, Izanami!" cried Izanagi. "An island."

As Izanami swirled, islands thickened in the churning water. Five great islands took shape among a scattering of smaller isles. These were the islands of Japan, their mountains cloaked with forests, their valleys bright with flowers and streams.

Izanami smiled. "Now we must make children to rule this beautiful world."

Izanagi nodded. He waded into the water. First, he washed his left eye. At once, a daughter was born, so bright that her father and mother had to shade their eyes. She was Amaterasu, goddess of the Sun.

Then Izanagi washed his right eye and a son was born, glowing with silvery light. This was Tsukuyomi, god of the Moon. Finally, Izanagi washed his nose. A second son was born, wailing and thrashing his arms and legs. This was Susanoo, god of the sea.

The children lived in the many-halled palace of heaven. Amaterasu and Tsukuyomi ruled together, side by side. Both the Sun and Moon shone in the sky at once, bathing the islands in their brilliant light through night and day.

When the first humans were born on the islands, Izanagi and Izanami decided it was time for another child. Their second daughter was Ukemochi, goddess of food. She gave humans as much fish, meat, fruit, and grain as they could eat.

As the young gods grew up, their parents delighted in their company, seeing the world anew through their eyes. And yet, one of the children so outshone the others that they could not help but become jealous. Amaterasu was brilliant in her intellect, charming company, a talented musician, and her radiant beauty was unmatched. Her parents adored her. As a result, Amaterasu grew increasingly vain, and Susanoo, in particular, became more and more bitter.

One day, Ukemochi invited her brothers and sister to a feast. Sullen Susanoo refused to attend. Amaterasu was too busy braiding her radiant hair to go, but she ordered Tsukuyomi to go and be polite.

When Tsukuyomi was seated at the long table in Ukemochi's hall, the goddess of food waved a gracious hand. "You are welcome, brother," she said.

Tsukuyomi looked at the bare table. He had been expecting a delicious feast worthy of an all-powerful god. Giving an impatient sigh, he began to tap his foot on the floor.

Ukemochi rolled up her sleeves. First, she dipped a finger in the ocean and, after a wet cough, pulled a plump fish from her mouth. Then she waved a hand through the forests and, after some spluttering, produced a bird, feathers and all, from behind her teeth. Next, she stroked a field of rice. Her shoulders heaved and she spat out a huge heap of rice. The goddess looked pleased with her feast.

Tsukuyomi was disgusted. His own stomach churned sickeningly. His sister had insulted him with this horrible display. He drew his sword and, with a flash of metal, killed Ukemochi.

Hearing the servants' wails, Amaterasu rushed to Ukemochi's hall. There stood Tsukuyomi beside his sister's body, his guilty sword still in his hand.

Amaterasu shook with grief and horror. "What have you done?" she screamed. "How can you just stand there? Get out! Get out! I never want to see you again."

Lost in shame, Tsukuyomi shuffled from the palace. From that moment, Amaterasu and Tsukuyomi never looked on each other's faces again. Tsukoyomi ruled the night, his light dimmed by his sorrow. Amaterasu blazed during the day.

Alone beside her sister's body, Amaterasu was sorry she had been too busy paying attention to her hair to be there for her family, and she knew she must act to carry on Ukemochi's work. Without Ukemochi to provide for them, the people of the islands would starve. Amaterasu ran her fingers through her poor sister's hair, pulling out oxen and horses. From Ukemochi's nostrils, she picked millet seeds, from her belly button she plucked rice, from between her toes she collected wheat. From her sister's mouth, Amaterasu pulled threads of silk spun by busy silkworms. Then Amaterasu sowed the millet seeds across the islands of Japan. She sent oxen and horses to gallop across the valleys. She placed each wriggling silkworm in a mulberry tree.

This was how Amaterasu gave the skills of farming and silk-making to the people of Japan. As long as Amaterasu could manage to keep the world in order, humans would never be hungry or cold.

To still her sad, fluttering heart, Amaterasu sat down at her weaving loom. She loved to weave cloth as fine and soft as clouds. The goddess began to pass her wooden shuttle to and fro between the evenly spaced threads, pulling its tail of thread behind it. The careful movement began to calm her.

With a cry and a wail, in burst her brother Susanoo, angry tears running down his cheeks. "It's all your fault!" he shouted. "If you hadn't been too selfish to go to the feast, my sister wouldn't be dead. My brother wouldn't be gone."

"I wish they were both still here, Susanoo," answered Amaterasu, trying to keep her voice from shaking.

Susanoo stamped his foot so hard that the shuttle fell from Amaterasu's hand. "You've always thought you were better than the rest of us!" he yelled.

This was too much. "Leave me alone!" shouted Amaterasu.

And with a slam of the door, Susanoo was gone. Amaterasu sighed and picked up her shuttle.

As she worked, Amaterasu heard the wind start to howl outside. It battered the palace walls, clattering the roof tiles and rattling the gates.

"Oh, stop it, Susanoo ..." groaned Amaterasu.

Now came the rain, pouring so hard and so fast that water curled under the doors to soak mats and table legs. There were shouts in the corridor, the sound of galloping hooves—and in burst Susanoo on the back of a terrifying horse, its eyes rolling and its nostrils flaring.

The horse was galloping straight at Amaterasu! Before she could scramble to her feet, the horse hurtled into her loom, splintering wood and ripping threads. The shuttle hit Amaterasu in the face. She tumbled backward onto the floor, her legs flying helplessly over her head.

"Hah!" yelled Susanoo. "Not so perfect now, are you?"

In ran the servants, just in time to see Amaterasu lying in a messy heap on the floor, her clothes in disarray. She thought she heard someone snigger.

Amaterasu stood up and smoothed out her clothes. She was burning with anger and humiliation. The servants were staring at her. Susanoo was smirking. She wanted to say something to cut Susanoo down to size, to make him pay for shaming her in front of the servants. But all that came into her head was that everyone thought she was in the wrong, and everyone thought she was pathetic. No one was on her side.

She turned and ran.

Amaterasu ran out of the palace and into the mountains. She wanted to be where no one could see her. She ran into the cave where she and Tsukuyomi used to play. She pulled a rock in front of the entrance, sealing herself inside. Now she let the tears come.

Outside, the world was plunged into darkness. Tsukuyomi's ghostly gleam was not enough to light the way, to warm the fields, to keep children safe. Everyone was afraid. People hid in their homes, clutching each other's hands and crying: "Where is the Sun? What have we done to deserve this? Whatever shall we do?"

After three days of darkness, the gods and goddesses gathered outside Amaterasu's cave. They called to the goddess: "People are lost and frightened, Amaterasu. Please come out," they begged.

Amaterasu felt even more ashamed. How could she come out when she had done so much harm? She would have to say sorry to the whole world. She stayed inside the cave.

The gods and goddesses tried tricks to lure Amaterasu out. Amo-no-Azume, goddess of laughter, kicked over a bucket outside the cave. Crashing the bucket against the rock, she danced and leaped. The other gods laughed.

Hearing the laughter, Amaterasu was certain that people were making fun of her. She stayed inside the cave.

Omoikane, the god of wisdom, stepped forward. He knew that Amaterasu's chief fault was that she was vain. But he also knew that, more than anything, she wanted to be useful. "Amaterasu," he called at the rock door. "Don't worry, you can stay where you are. An even more beautiful goddess has come to light the world."

Amaterasu gasped. The world did not need her! Could there really be a brighter goddess? She pushed back the stone, just a crack, and peeped out.

"Here," said Omoikane, putting something in her hand. "Take a look."

Amaterasu looked at what Omoikane had given her. She saw a lovely face streaked with dirt and tears. Omoikane had handed her a mirror.

Amo-no-Azume pulled Amaterasu out of the cave and, quick as they could, the gods rolled back the stone and tied it with rope.

"Nobody's laughing at you," whispered Amo-no-Azume. She squeezed Amaterasu's hand. "We're here to help. Even the greatest goddess needs friends."

Amaterasu was sorry for having deprived the world of her light, but she knew she must get back to work. She would never again let others' jealousy of her beauty and talent cast the world into darkness. And from the day to this, the Sun has shone on the islands of Japan, taking it in turns with her brother the Moon.

Isis Discovers the Name of Ra

Based on Egyptian myths

Before our world began, there was only swirling water in the darkness. Then, a name was whispered over the crash of the waves. It was a secret name that brought a god to life. The god never told anyone else his secret name, for it would grant them power over him. Instead, he was known as Ra, god of the Sun.

Ra had the sharp beak and bristling feathers of a falcon. His crown bore the symbol of his power—the circle of the Sun. Ra's rays dried the land and separated water from the sky. Ra gave life to all things, from beetles to crocodiles, humans to jackals, by speaking their names. Every day, Ra guided the Sun across the sky, warming the fields. At dusk, he stepped into the underworld. All night, Ra fought his way through the underworld's shifting slippery dangers. Yet every morning, he found his way back to the surface, carrying the Sun with him.

Ra had many children, who had many children of their own. One of Ra's great grandchildren, Isis, loved to watch the aged god on his daily walk. She longed to speak to him, but Ra was proud and quick to anger. Isis did not dare to disturb him.

As the years went by, Isis noticed that Ra's steps slowed. His back bowed under the weight of his burden. His once bright feathers were pale and dull.

Ra no longer had the strength to lift the Sun high in the sky. Now, the fiery ball barely skimmed the tops of the mountains. Sitting lower to the Earth meant its fierce heat was much stronger. It cracked the mud and frazzled the trees. The streams dried up, their water sizzling into steam.

No rain fell on Egypt's parched crops. Where there were once gardens, now there was desert. Before, the wind had gently rustled leaves and petals, now it blew up blinding sandstorms. People were hungry and thirsty. They hid from the Sun as best they could beneath bare branches.

The gods and goddesses were worried. A group of them went to Ra and asked him to let them carry the Sun instead.

Spitting with fury, Ra banished the gods from his sight. Perhaps he knew in his heart that the gods were right, but the truth was a heavier burden for him to bear than the Sun itself.

Isis watched the hungry children crouching in the dust. She watched their parents searching the desert for water. Isis began to cry.

Once her tears started to fall, Isis could not stop them. Tears ran down her cheeks and dripped onto the ground. Her pool of tears grew deeper. A trickle broke from the pool's edge and snaked across the dry ground. Gathering strength, the stream became a river. The wide river surged all the way to the distant sea.

Shouting with joy, the people of Egypt scooped water to drink. They dug channels to carry the river's water to their fields. Children splashed and played in the shallows as glinting fish swam between their legs. They gave Isis's river a name—the Nile.

Yet while Ra still stumbled across the Earth, the people of Egypt were not safe. Isis knew that Ra would never willingly give up the Sun. Ra gained all his power from the secret name that Nu had whispered to him in the first moment. No one but Ra knew this name. Nothing would make Ra speak it, for if anyone knew this secret, he would be at their mercy. Isis had an idea.

Hiding herself behind a rock, Isis waited beside the path that Ra took across the Earth. Soon she heard Ra muttering to himself bad-temperedly. Isis peeped out.

"So the other gods think they can do better!" grumbled Ra. "When they have walked the Earth as long as I have ..." Ra spat with disgust, his spittle flying onto the mud. When Isis was sure that Ra was out of sight, she scooped up the mud soaked with the god's spit. She rolled the mud between her hands, shaping it into a snake. Pinching with her fingertips, she fashioned the snake's sharp fangs and beady eyes. Then she whispered the snake's name, giving it life. Its scales glittered as it wriggled in Isis's lap. The snake was the same shade as the sandy floor that it slithered across on its belly.

The next day, when Ra came walking by, he did not see the snake curled across his path. Opening its jaws wide, the snake sank its fangs into Ra's heel.

Ra yelled as the snake's poison quickly did its work. The god fell to the ground, grabbing at his foot and writhing with pain.

Isis ran out from her hiding place. "Grandfather, what is it?" she cried. "Has a snake bitten you? How could a snake dare to do such a thing?"

Shuddering, Ra groaned: "It burns like wildfire! I've never felt such awful pain. Poison is roaring through my veins."

"Great Grandfather," said Isis, kneeling at his side. "You must tell me your secret name. You will live if I can only speak your name."

Clutching at the air, Ra moaned: "I'm shivering with cold! I cannot see!"

"Tell me your secret name, quickly," gasped Isis, shocked at what she had done. She grabbed her grandfather's shaking hand.

"Oh, I am the maker of Earth and Heaven, of gods and humans, of animals and plants, of light and dark."

"I know, I know all that. But what's your secret name?" begged Isis.

The old god huffed as he said "Oh, I am Ra when the Sun is high. At dawn, I am Khepri as I roll the Sun onto the Earth like a beetle rolls a ball of dung. At dusk, I am Atum as I wage war against the powers of night."

"No, no, Grandfather" said Isis, "I know those names already. Everybody does. It's your secret name I need."

"Granddaughter," panted Ra, his voice so weak that Isis had to lean forward to catch his words, "I cannot tell you that name. Nu whispered it to me. I buried it in my breast, where it must stay hidden. If it is known, chaos will reign."

"Grandfather, trust me, please," urged Isis, her eyes wide. "I promise that I will keep your secret name safe."

Ra looked into Isis's face. He had seen her many times on his daily walk. He had often wished she might keep him company, but she never came near.

With the last of his breath, Ra whispered his secret name into Isis's ear.

At once, Isis recited a spell:

"Let the poison fail, let the poison fall,

May Ra live, king of the gods,

Poison flow from his blood, pain flow from his bones,

May Ra live, king of the gods,

For he has given me his name, given me his power,

May Ra live, king of the gods."

Then, very quietly, Isis whispered Ra's secret name.

Ra stopped shaking. Isis wiped the sweat from his forehead. When Ra was ready, Isis helped him to his feet. Together, they walked the rest of the path, but it was Isis who now held the Sun aloft, high above the fields and mountains.

From that day forward, the task of guarding the Sun belonged to Isis. Soaring through the air on her feathered wings, she wore a crown that bore the symbol of her power—the circle of the Sun. Isis often asked Ra to join her on her daily journey so she could listen to his stories. She loved to hear about the day when Ra made humans from his sweat. She urged Ra to tell about his victories against evil Apep, the enemy of light and order. The best story of all was how Ra turned himself into a cat and caught Apep in his sharp claws.

As Isis worked carefully, the Earth cooled, plants flourished, and the people of Egypt rejoiced. Once every year, the Nile flooded the fields along its banks, giving them rich black soil to feed the crops for the coming year. People built tall, pillared temples to worship the great goddess Isis. They thanked Isis for her tears and for her daring plan to discover the secret name of Ra.

Sedna
of the Sea

Based on Inuit myths

O nce upon a time, in the far, snowy, north of the world lived a girl named
Sedna. One of the things she liked to do best was to carve little figurines.
Today, despite the cold wind whipping her fingers, she was carving one for
her father. She blew on her hands to warm them, then returned to scraping firmly with
her knife. Her latest carving was a seal with flippers that looked ready to swim away.
Sedna loved all animals, but she loved sea creatures best of all. The bone carving was a
gift for her father, Ataata. Before he went hunting tomorrow, Ataata would put the little
seal in the pocket of his anorak. Feeling the sculpture close to his heart, he would not
forget that each animal had its own soul. Every Inuit hunter knew that, without respect
for those souls, he and his family would go hungry.

A dog howled, setting off a chorus by the other village dogs. The dogs were nervous
tonight.

Sedna sank her cold hands into her pockets. Looking out over the sea ice, she saw
the last hunters returning on their sleds, pulled along by dogs racing toward a well-earned

reward. Sedna dropped to her knees and crawled into her family's igloo. She was greeted by the hot, rich smell of stew. Her mother was stirring a pot over the oil lamp.

"For you, Ataata," said Sedna, handing her father the bone seal.

"Ah, it's very beautiful," said her father, admiring her handiwork. "It looks so alive I wouldn't be surprised if it leaped from my hand and dived for shrimp!"

"Can I come hunting tomorrow?" asked Sedna.

Ataata frowned. "Not tomorrow." He cleared his throat nervously. "Your mother and I need to talk to you." He looked at Sedna's mother for support.

Sedna's mother put her hands on her hips. "Sedna," she said firmly. "You have turned down every young hunter in this village and the next. But it's time you chose a husband." She wagged her spoon, spattering the furs with gravy. "A very fine hunter has come to the village looking for a wife. And we ..." She bit her lip. "We have invited him for dinner."

"But ..." gasped Sedna. "I don't want to get married. I want to hunt for myself. I want to travel to the other side of the ocean. I want to—"

A dog howled close by.

"Aluu," called a strange voice outside.

Before Sedna had time to say more, in crawled the hunter, bringing with him a blast of cold air. When the hunter pushed back his hood, Sedna saw the most handsome face she could ever have imagined. His bright eyes glittered, his hair shone, his nose was so straight it was almost sharp.

The hunter gave Sedna a dazzling smile and she found herself smiling back.

And so it was arranged. Before Sedna knew it, she was climbing into the hunter's kayak and waving goodbye to her weeping parents. Her mother and father grew smaller and smaller until she could no longer see them between the white sea and sky.

Sedna watched the hunter's back as he paddled them toward his island. His arms were long and strong, even longer than she remembered.

"Is it far?" she asked him a little nervously. This was all so new, so strange. She could hardly remember how she had come to be here.

The hunter turned his head, his nose sharp against the light. "Not much farther."

The hunter paddled onward, his arms seeming to grow ever longer. Sedna knew it was only her imagination that made his arms seem to bend and stretch like flapping wings.

The hunter threw back his hood. His hair bristled down his back. Sedna's breath caught in her throat. She reached out a shaking hand. This was not hair. It was feathers. Wiry feathers.

"Wait ... Stop ..." What was happening?

The hunter turned, his nose a beak, his arms opening wider and wider—into wings.

Sedna scrambled to get away, and fell overboard. The enormous bird plucked her anorak in its beak and lifted her from the water. The bird carried Sedna over the ocean, higher and higher, her arms and legs waving helplessly in the air.

An island was drawing closer, its black rocks jagged against the sky. At last, the bird set Sedna down on a narrow rock ledge. She found herself in a nest of twigs and moss. Sedna's husband was a fulmar bird, a qaqulluk.

The qaqulluk flapped around Sedna, watching her out of a beady eye. Shivering shook Sedna's bones and chattered her teeth. Hot tears burned her icy cheeks. She wrapped her arms tightly around herself. She and her parents had been horribly tricked. Far below, the waves foamed against the dark rocks. If Sedna leaned too far over the edge of her ledge, she would tumble into the icy water. She was trapped. When the qaqulluk was certain that Sedna had accepted her fate, it flew away. It soared over the ocean, swooping every so often to snatch a fish.

For hour after hour, there was nothing to do but watch the waves. As darkness started to fall, Sedna saw something. A kayak had washed up on the island. It was wedged between two rocks and still had paddles on the inside. If Sedna could climb down, she could get herself home.

"F-chee!" The qaqulluk gave a cackling call as it landed on the edge of the nest.

The bird dropped a wet fish in Sedna's lap. She knew that if she was going to escape, she must eat. She bit into the salty flesh, choking it down her dry throat. Sedna's husband perched beside her on the ledge, preening his feathers with his beak.

In the darkness of that long night, Sedna rested her head on the twigs of her prison. She thought of her bone sculptures. She had loved to carve seals, walruses, fish, and whales. How she longed to be free like those creatures, free to swim far and wide.

When the sun peeped above the horizon, the qaqulluk took flight again, leaving Sedna alone in the nest. Now was her chance.

Lying on her stomach, Sedna stretched her legs over the edge of the cliff, reaching for a foothold with her toes. Her feet found a shelf of rock. She let herself slip down, then, clinging with her fingers, stretched for a lower ledge. Scraping her knees and banging her elbows, Sedna edged down the cliff. At last, she jumped into the tossing kayak. She grabbed the paddle and pulled it hard through the water, dipping it left then right, left then right. With every stroke, she was farther from her prison.

"F-chee!" The qaqulluk swooped, its beak pecking at her anorak.

"Go away!" she yelled, waving her paddle over her head. "Let me go!"

The qaqulluk swerved and flapped, stirring up great waves, raising a fierce wind with the force of its wings. The kayak bucked and fell, tipping Sedna sideways and tumbling her head first into the icy water. Somersaulting fast, she pulled to the surface and managed to grab the side of the kayak with one hand.

The furious qaqulluk beat its terrible wings harder and faster. Sedna gripped the swinging kayak with four frozen fingers. If she let go, the weight of her furs would pull her to the bottom of the ocean.

The qaqulluk darted at Sedna, its beak open wide. It was going to pluck her from the water and carry her back to its nest like a fish. Sedna couldn't bear to be parted from her beloved sea, to live high up in the sky. Anything was better than that. Gritting her teeth, Sedna let her numb fingers lose their grip on the kayak and she sank beneath the water.

The sea embraced her in its icy waters like an old friend. As she sank deeper and deeper, something strange happened to her frozen fingers. Her first finger changed into a long-tusked walrus. Her second finger became a seal. Her third finger turned into a stout whale. And her fourth finger was transformed into a shoal of shimmering fish.

Sedna's furs floated away and she saw she had grown a shining blue tail. Now all the sea's creatures swam to greet Sedna, their goddess. They wove themselves between the strands of her flowing hair. The seals nuzzled her cheek. The whales sang her their long, low songs. Flicking her gorgeous tail, Sedna swam joyfully among them, free forever from the qaqulluk, free to swim wherever she pleased.

Since that day, whenever an Inuit hunter shows respect for the animals of the sea, Sedna frees a creature from her endless hair and lets it swim to the surface. But when a hunter tries to take more animals than they truly need, Sedna becomes angry. Then she refuses to release any animal until the Inuit comfort her with stories of a brave girl who wanted to be free. Today, Sedna is angered by the strangers who take more from the ocean than they could ever need. Perhaps if we tell Sedna's story, she will be comforted still.

Pandora
and the Jar

Based on Greek myths

Long ago, Greece was watched over by a group of gods and goddesses, who lived up in the clouds, at the top of the enormous Mount Olympus. Zeus, king of the gods, had created mankind and given them a perfect world to enjoy.

Zeus's wife, Hera, wasn't sure that he had done the right thing. When she looked down, she could see the men safe in the garden that Zeus had planted for them. They played, sang, and ate fruit from the trees. They had nothing to fear and yet they didn't seem completely happy.

"They are bored," Hera grumbled to herself. "Humans need to learn, build, and work for things to be truly happy. I know exactly what to do."

Hephaestus knew better than to question his mother. The young god kneeled on the wet ground, scooped up handfuls of sticky mud—and set to work. His hands moved quickly as he formed a leg, an elbow, a rib, and the curve of an ear.

Aphrodite, the goddess of love, walked into the workshop.

Hephaestus smiled shyly at the beautiful goddess. "I'm glad you've come, Aphrodite.

I'm making a woman for the garden of men. I will model her face on yours."

Aphrodite smiled. "It would be more useful to make her strong."

Blushing a little, Hephaestus nodded. Carefully now, with the tips of his fingers, he curved eyebrows, squeezed the tip of a nose, hollowed the dip of a chin.

Now Zeus strode into the room. "What are you making?" he asked. The other gods and goddesses trooped in behind their king. They had just returned from a hunting trip. They looked dusty and sweaty.

Hera drew herself up to her full height. "You're just in time. We are making a girl to join the men below." As Zeus's mouth began to open, Hera raised a firm and queenly hand. "And she is in need of breath. Where are the Anemoi?"

"We're here!" chorused the four gods of the wind. They squeezed through the crowd: Boreas, god of the north wind; Zephyrus, god of the west wind; Notus, god of the south wind; and Eurus, god of the east wind.

Leaning close, the four gods blew in the face of the sculpted girl. The mud quivered—and with a cough the girl took her first breath. Her eyes opened. They were fringed with lashes so delicate it was hard to believe that Hephaestus had made them with his rough fingers. The girl gazed around her. Trembling, she clenched her fingers into fists.

Hera laid a hand on the girl's shoulder. "Be brave, Daughter"

"Well," said Zeus, clapping his hands. "If she's to join my men, we must give her some skills." He looked at the assembled gods, then beckoned Hermes.

Hermes, the swift-footed messenger of the gods, stepped forward. "I give her the gift of speech," he said, waving a hand toward the girl's mouth.

Now Zeus gestured to Apollo, the cheerful god of music and dancing. Flourishing a hand, Apollo sang: "I give her the gift of playing the lyre, so she will always make sweet music."

"Good," said Zeus. "And I—" he pointed at the girl "—give her the gift of laughter. Now," he said, turning on his heel, "a cooling dip in the sea is in order after all this very hard work."

The chattering gods and goddesses followed their king from the room. Hera stayed

still, her hand on the girl. To Hera's relief, she saw that three of the goddesses had remained: Athena, Aphrodite, and Peitho.

Hera nodded to Athena, the towering goddess of war and wisdom.

The fierce goddess stepped forward. In one hand she gripped a shining spear, and on her shoulder perched an owl, its bright eyes all-seeing. Athena put a heavy hand on the girl's head. "Girl, I give you the gift of wisdom."

"Thank you," said the girl. Her sweet voice was surprisingly firm.

Aphrodite very gently touched the girl's chest. "And I give you the gift of love, kindness, and generosity.

The girl smiled, daring to look into the goddess's shining face.

It was Peitho's turn. The goddess of persuasion touched the girl's cheek lightly with her fingers. "I give you the great gift of knowing the difference between right and wrong."

The girl nodded gravely.

"Finally, precious daughter," said Hera, "I give you the gift of curiosity."

The other goddesses murmured their approval.

"But what is my name?" asked the girl.

Hera looked thoughtful. "I think we will call you Pandora. It means 'every gift.'"

Taking Pandora by the hand, Hera led her down the slopes of Mount Olympus into the garden of men. There she left the girl alone.

Pandora could hear laughter. Eager to meet her new companions, she skipped in the direction of the noise. Lounging in the shade of trees heavy with pears and figs were twenty men and boys. One braided a garland of red flowers while another plucked the strings of a lyre. Three or four dozed in the sunshine, bees buzzing harmlessly above their heads.

When the men saw Pandora, they stared in astonishment. The lyre fell to the ground.

Pandora swallowed hard. "The gods have sent me to join you," she explained, trying to keep her voice certain and steady.

"Then you are very welcome!" cried one of the men. "My name is Prometheus." He shook her hand excitedly.

"And I am Epimetheus," said another. "Would you like a pear?" He offered her a soft, ripe fruit.

And so Pandora settled into life in the world of men. All day, and every day, they sang and danced in the sunlight. At night, they gathered in the pavilions that Zeus had built for them. Gentle breezes wafted between the marble pillars to lull them to sleep. There was no need to fear the darkness or a hungry wolf because Zeus had made nothing that could harm them. No one argued or spoke unkindly. Pandora should have been blissfully happy.

The problem was that Pandora was soon bored. Nothing in the garden ever changed. Every song was as tuneful as the last. Every fruit as ripe as any other. Pandora started to long for something new, something different. She began to wonder what lay over the next hill, behind the next grove. One day, as she explored far from the others, she came across

a circular pavilion she had never noticed before. On the pavilion's steps was a jar.

Pandora knew at once that the jar was special. It was made of baked clay, its surface painted with a bright and intricate pattern. She had never seen the men make anything like it. Yet skilled hands had spent many hours creating this jar. She wondered what was inside. She put her hand on the lid.

"Stop!" yelled a voice. Epimetheus was sprinting toward her. "Don't open it!"

"Why not?" gasped Pandora. Epimetheus looked frightened. But why was he frightened when there was nothing in the world to fear?

"Zeus told us not to," stammered Epimetheus. "It's the one thing we're not allowed to do. We mustn't ever open the jar."

"But ..." said Pandora, running her fingers over the jar's lid. "What is it doing here if we're not allowed to open it?"

"Come away," begged Epimetheus, leading Pandora back to the others.

Yet the next day, when no one was looking, Pandora returned to the jar. She traced

her fingers over its pattern. She lifted it to test its weight. She pressed her ear to its side. Something in the jar was fluttering. What could it be? What was inside?

Pandora had to know. Without giving herself a chance to change her mind, she lifted the lid and looked inside. Something dark was crouching there. She scrambled backward, but not fast enough—a black shape burst into her face, knocking her back. The thing was free, flapping into the air on black wings.

"I bring sickness!" roared the thing.

A second black creature flapped from the jar, its slick wings brushing sickeningly against Pandora's face. "I bring death!" it hissed.

Pandora tried to slam the lid back on the jar—but it was too late! Four more monsters were squeezing out into the world, their wings spreading wide: "I bring war! I bring cruelty! I bring hate! I bring lies!" the flying beasts chanted.

Pandora sobbed. She shook with fear and grief. What had she done to the world? There was no way of getting the evil back into the jar, not ever.

But something else was peeping from the jar. A small creature fluttered hesitantly out, its pale wings so filmy they seemed too weak to fly.

Pandora slowly stretched out her hand. The little creature landed on her fingertip. It glimmered faintly. Pandora cupped her other hand around the creature, as if she was protecting a spark in the wind. The creature glowed brighter.

"I bring hope," whispered the little creature. It spoke so quietly that Pandora could almost not have heard.

"Then not everything is lost," said Pandora, cradling the fragile creature. "I will keep you safe. I promise." She dried her tears.

High above, on Mount Olympus, Hera and Zeus walked arm in arm. Zeus sighed sadly, wiping a hand across his eyes.

Hera squeezed her husband's hand. "This is how it has to be, my love. Life may be hard for them now, but they have things to do and achieve," she said. "And they will always have hope."

Nüwa and the Pillars of Heaven

Based on Chinese myths

At first, there was nothing. Then the universe began with the cracking of a great egg. Out of the egg crawled Pangu, a horned giant. Pangu was really, really hairy. From Pangu's body sprang everything that we know—his right eye became the moon, his left eye the sun, his muscles the land, his blood the rivers, his fur the forests, his breath the wind. His four limbs became the pillars that hold up the sky. From Pangu's fur hopped fleas that became extraordinary beings.

Among those beings were Nüwa and her brother Fuxi. They had bright eyes, clever hands, and brave hearts. Beneath their robes curled long, snaking tails. The sister and brother lived on Mount Kunlun. They were all alone, with only the whistling winds and winter snows for company. Nüwa grew lonelier and lonelier.

Every day, Nüwa went down to the plains below. Today, those plains are home to farms and cities, but these were the days before people were created. Nüwa fed nuts to the deer and helped the cranes build their nests. But she still felt lonely.

One day, as Nüwa was walking beside the Yellow River, she caught sight of her own reflection in the water. For a moment, her heart burst with pleasure. What joy to see another face! If only there were truly another being like herself so she could talk with them. Then Nüwa had an idea. She would make beings that looked just like her and Fuxi, so they would never be alone again.

She kneeled on the muddy riverbank. Working painstakingly for many hours, Nüwa scooped handful after handful of mud, rolling and pinching each into the shape of a man or woman. Although Nüwa was fond of her tail, she chose to make her people without them. Gently and lovingly, she breathed life into every one of her mud people.

Nüwa was delighted with what she had done. From her palace on Mount Kunlun, she could watch her people build homes, sow seeds, and raise children. Whenever she was tired of Fuxi's company, she hid her tail beneath her dress and descended to the plain, where she was welcomed with bowls of noodles and platters of jujubes or bayberries.

Yet Nüwa and her brother were not the only beings that had hopped from Pangu's thick fur. Splashing in the rivers and oceans was the water god Gonggong. Wherever his scaly tail grazed the ground, a spring burst from the rock. Flying on his fierce tiger was the fire god Zhurong. Whenever it pleased Zhurong, he touched his flaming torch to dry trees and grasses, sending beasts and people fleeing in terror. These two gods were bitter enemies. Each longed to claim the Throne of Heaven for himself.

"You are powerless against me!" spat Gonggong as he passed Zhurong in the clouds. With a flick of his tail, Gonggong drenched his rival.

"I'll show you who's powerless," roared Zhurong, waving his torch across the rice fields that Gonggong had watered. The plants wilted and the ground cracked.

This was too much for Gonggong to bear. He flew head first into Zhurong, throwing the god from his tiger and choking him with icy waves. Yet Zhurong was strong and ruthless. He sprang back onto his tiger and thrust his torch in Gonggong's face, singeing his blue scales. Gonggong howled and writhed in pain, blindly trying to escape the tiger's vicious scratches. A cloud of scalding steam wrapped around the struggling gods.

Gonggong glimpsed a chance to use his most dangerous weapon—his tail. He curled it around Zhurong, pulling it tighter and tighter until the fire god plummeted toward the ground like a rock on a string. But the falling god dragged Gonggong down with him, sending both gods smashing into the earth.

Water surged from the broken ground, bubbling into a wave that grew and gained strength. As the wave raced across the fields, Nüwa's people grabbed their children and ran for high ground. Alas, the mountainsides were burning from the touch of Zhurong's torch, so there was no safe place for the humans.

"Stop! Stop it!" cried Nüwa as she flew down the slopes of Mount Kunlun.

Deafened by their anger, the two gods still wrestled, tumbling across the smoking, seething earth. Arms flailing and tails flying, they flipped over and over—hurtling into one of the four pillars that held up the sky. The crash was the loudest sound that was ever heard, before or since.

A crack appeared in the pillar, spreading from one side to the other. First with a crumble of dust, then with an avalanche of tumbling stone, the great support folded and fell. Her mouth open in horror, Nüwa could only watch as the sky, the sun, the moon, and stars all slipped sickeningly to the side. A great hole ripped across the sky itself. Sinking under the weight of the load, the land tipped dizzyingly to the southeast.

Desperate to escape the flood waters, Nüwa's people clung to the branches of trees, clambered up slippery slopes, and grasped for each other with shaking hands.

"Be gone!" yelled Nüwa at the dazed gods. "Neither of you deserves to be king. Learn to use your powers to help others, not to destroy!"

Shamed by their chaos, Gonggong and Zhurong slunk away without a word.

Nüwa wanted nothing more than to cry. But her people needed her. She rolled up her sleeves. Nüwa cupped the flood water in her hands and then trickled cooling rain over the burning forests. She scooped up the cinders of burned wood and sprinkled them where the water was deepest. The cinder piles swelled as they soaked up the flood. People began to climb down from their refuges.

Nüwa dusted off her hands. Her next task was to mend the hole in the sky. She

plucked five stones from the shallows, choosing one for each of the five elements that compose the universe. She chose a black stone for water, a white stone for metal, a yellow one for earth, a blue one for wood, and a red one for fire. She dropped the five stones into her cauldron, lit a fire, and then watched the stones melt. She stirred the thick, oozing liquid with her iron spoon. Pursing her lips with concentration, she carried a dripping spoonful right to the top of Mount Buzhou. The hole in the sky was just above her head. She used the special mixture she had made to patch the rent until it was as good as new.

Ever since that day, we can see the shades of Nüwa's stones in the sky. During the day, we see blue and white; at night, we see the deepest black. At sunrise and sunset, we can admire the traces of Nüwa's yellow and red pebbles.

Yet Nüwa's most difficult task remained. She had to find a way to prop up the sky.

"Ao!" called Nüwa, her voice echoing between mountains and spreading across the oceans. She flew across the world and back again, calling as loudly as she could: "Ao, come to me! Ao!"

Finally, deep beneath the waves of the ocean, the great turtle Ao heard her call. Pulling through the water with his scaly flippers, Ao swam to the surface.

When Nüwa saw Ao's beak rising through the ocean foam, she laughed with relief. "Thank you, Ao. I need your help. Your task is a hard one, but I know you are strong enough. Please come with me."

Nüwa positioned Ao so that each of his four limbs rested on the peak of a towering mountain. The turtle braced himself, then Nüwa stretched the sky across his broad shell. Ao bravely took the weight—and has held it ever since. Nüwa often keeps him company, stroking his rough cheek. Together, the goddess and turtle watch people at work and play on the plains below. Nüwa and Ao still talk of the day when they saved the world from destruction.

And yet, all is not quite as it was before Gonggong and Zhurong's fight. The ground still slopes to the southeast, which is why—as you may have noticed—all China's great rivers flow in that direction.

Hina Journeys to the Moon

Based on Polynesian myths

It was Hina and her brother Ru who discovered all the islands of Polynesia. Hina and Ru were born on an island far to the west. They were children of the sky god Atea and his wife Hotu. Every day, little Hina walked along the shore and wondered what lay beyond the waves. She told her brother that, when they were big and strong enough, they would set sail in their canoe and discover the world. And, one morning, that is exactly what they did.

Hina and Ru packed their canoe, which they had named Te-apori, with plenty of food and water. They raised a sail of tough matting. Hina sat at the stern, holding a large paddle for steering. Ru gripped a smaller paddle to use when the wind dropped. Together, they sailed expertly across the tossing waves for many days and nights, through balmy afternoons and stormy mornings. This was how Hina became known as Hina-fa'auru-va'a, which means Hina-the-canoe-pilot.

Whenever Hina sighted a new land on the shimmering horizon, she would call out to her brother: "Look, Ru! Land is approaching! What island is it?"

Ru would call back a name and Hina would clap with joy. "Perfect!" This was how they named the islands of Tahiti and Moʻorea, Huahaine and Tahaʻa, Kaukura and Niau. They named each island, each cove, each cape.

On the island of Raʻiatea, Hina and Ru dragged their canoe up the beach. They lay on the sand, letting the Sun warm their aching limbs.

"Tomorrow, let's sail to the southwest," said Ru. "I think there are more islands in that direction."

"Hmmm," murmured Hina, letting sand trickle through her fingers. "More islands . I'd prefer to discover something different for a change."

"Like what?" scoffed Ru. "What else is there to discover?"

Annoyed, Hina propped herself up on an elbow. "Everything!" She waved a hand at the sand, the sea, the sky. "Like the Sun!"

"You can't travel to the Sun, Hina," laughed Ru.

"Can't I?" yelled Hina. "Just you watch me. I'll do it tomorrow."

All night, Hina lay awake listening to Ru's snores. In a fit of anger, she had sworn to do something truly impossible. Of course, there was no way she could travel to the Sun! She would have to back down and tell Ru he was right. He would never let her forget it.

When the Sun finally rose over the horizon, drops of rain splattered on Hina's face. She opened her mouth and drank. She felt Ru stirring beside her. Lifting higher, the Sun shone bravely through the rain. Hina watched as a rainbow appeared, arching between land and sky, a brilliant pathway of red and green, orange and blue.

"Ru! I know how to do it!"

"What?" murmured Ru, pushing away Hina's prodding hand.

"I'll walk to the Sun along that rainbow! Quick, before it disappears."

She sprinted along the beach to where the rainbow dipped into the foaming surf. Without giving herself a moment to change her mind, Hina scrambled onto the rainbow.

"No, Hina! It's dangerous!" shouted Ru.

The rainbow bounced a little beneath Hina's bare feet, but it took her weight. Hina started to run, higher and higher, along the gleaming path of light. Startled seabirds flapped

around her. Far below, she could hear Ru's worried shouts, but he was growing smaller and smaller. With every step, it was getting hotter. The Sun was scorching her skin. She put up a hand to shield her face. Sweat prickled on her scalp and trickled into her smarting eyes. Hina looked down. The island was no more than a smudge on the blue sea. She felt herself sway. She stretched out her arms, trying to steady herself. She looked ahead, toward the blazing Sun, but it was too bright, too fierce. She squeezed her eyes shut. Even through her eyelids, she could see the Sun's orange glare. Hina started to sob.

Ru was right. This was too dangerous. She turned and ran, back down the rainbow, running faster and faster as Ru grew bigger and bigger. Then her feet were on damp sand and Ru was hugging her.

"I've been stupid. I've failed," she said through her tears.

"It's not stupid to try something and fail. That's how we learn," said Ru kindly.

But Hina still hungered to journey somewhere new, somewhere that no one else had ever been, somewhere no one would even dare to dream of. That night, as she watched the Moon peep over the edge of the dark ocean, Hina had an idea.

"Ru, let me borrow the canoe," she gasped.

"Hang on, Hina ..." said Ru tiredly.

Without waiting to hear another word, Hina leaped into Te-apori and raised the sail. She must be quick or the Moon would rise above the horizon. Hina-fa'auru-va'a steered along the Moon's silvery trail across the waves. Not a moment too soon, the canoe bumped the Moon's dusty edge and Hina leaped out. And this was how Hina became known as Hina-i-aa-i-te-marama, which means Hina-who-stepped-into-the-Moon.

She pushed the canoe back toward her brother. "Go back to Ru, Te-apori," she ordered. "And give him all my love," she added, her voice cracking at the thought that she was all alone now for the first time in her life.

Hina decided to make herself busy. She soon realized that the Moon's dark shadows, which we can see from Earth, are actually the branches of a banyan tree. Hina wanted to try something new. She set herself the difficult task of making cloth from the bark of this tree.

She stripped bark from a few of the tree's many trunks, for the banyan is not content with just one trunk like an ordinary tree. Examining her bark strips closely, Hina decided to rip away the outer bark, which was too tough for cloth. She dried the inner bark in the sunlight before soaking it in water for a while. Then, using an anvil and a mallet, she beat the bark pulp into a long, thin strip. She decided to call her cloth tapa.

As she beat her tapa, Hina liked to make rhythms with her mallet, then sing along with her own tunes, telling the story of her adventures with Ru:

"Look, Ru! Land is approaching! What island is it?" she sang.

Finally, Hina painted her tapa with zigzagging mountains, curling waves, fish, and birds. She made her paints using turmeric, soot, and candlenut sap that she collected.

Before long, all the gods and goddesses who watched over the Earth and visited the Moon, were asking Hina for her beautiful tapa to wear as dresses and robes. And this is how Hina gained the name of Hina-tutu-ha'a, which means Hina-the-cloth-beater.

While Hina worked in the Moon, she watched her beloved brother set sail to the southwest, where he soon discovered the great islands he dreamed of. Hina shouted her congratulations to Ru, who—never content to be still—soon set sail again.

Before long, Ru and Hina's route across the ocean was followed by men, women, and children in rocking canoes. When these brave people were lost on the wide ocean, Hina pointed the way. To this day, the people of Polynesia sing songs in praise of Hina-nui-te-araara, Hina-the-watchwoman, who directed them to a safe cove when the waves were high.

Now Hina decided she should share her tapa-making skills with the people below. Yet no banyan trees grew on the islands of Polynesia. Hina had an idea. A plump green pigeon lived in the branches of Hina's banyan, where it ate the tree's figs and cooed to itself. Hina called the pigeon to her.

Placing a branch of ripe figs in the bird's beak, Hina gave strict instructions: "Little pigeon, please carry these figs to every island, from Tahiti to Niau, so people can make tapa and find shelter beneath banyan branches."

The pigeon fluttered over the sparkling ocean, grasping the banyan branch firmly in its yellow beak. Just as the bird was readying to drop the first fig, a fierce frigate bird swooped, seizing the branch with its hooked beak. The frigate bird rarely took the trouble to hunt for its own food. Selfish and lazy, it preferred to steal from other birds. The frigate bird tussled and tugged, but the determined pigeon held firm, flapping its green wings

as hard as it could. Pulled between the two birds, the branch cracked—and snapped, scattering figs to the four winds. The figs plummeted, spinning and tumbling, onto each of the islands below.

The figs were caught by the stretching branches of island trees, where the banyan seeds found dark crevices and sent out their first shoots. The banyan saplings began to grow roots, which reached down from their tree branches, through the air, to the damp soil far below. As the banyan trees grew bigger, they sent down root after root, which thickened into trunks so wide that no one could tell which trunk had been the first. Over hundreds of years, Hina's banyans grew as tall as twenty-five people. Beneath the banyans' sheltering branches, the people of Polynesia talked, sang, and beat tapa.

Tanis and the Windigo

Based on Ojibwe myths

A long time ago, in the land that we now know as North America, a girl called Tanis crunched through fresh winter snow. She turned to admire her trail of perfect, even footprints. The pawprints of her puppies, Zaagi and Mino, wound among her footsteps, making loops and sudden playful zigzags.

"Good boy, Zaagi," she said, patting her puppy's shaggy head. He snuffled at her hand, warming her cold fingers with his damp breath.

Now Mino bounded up, wetting her skirt with his soggy feet. He sniffed urgently at Tanis's pocket. "You want lunch already? I'm hungry, too. But Grandma has asked us to collect sumac. We must do that before we eat," she said firmly. She tousled Mino's fur.

Here was a sumac bush, its red berries bright as flames among the snow and the dark, leafless trees. The spears of berries seemed like the only living things in the forest. Through the long, cold winter, Tanis and Grandma could eat the berries. Grandma also knew how to make tea from sumac leaves to cure the village's coughs. She would boil the shrub's roots and twigs to make a paste for hunters' wounds.

Tanis plucked berries and twigs, placing them carefully in her bag. Her belly was grumbling with hunger, but Grandma was relying on her to bring back a full bag.

There was a flutter of red feathers among the branches. It was an opichi, an American robin. It was small and alone, its feathers ruffled.

"You've stayed late in the year, little opichi. You should have flown south," Tanis chided gently as the bird stared at the berries in her hand. She knew hunger when she saw it. Her own belly gave a painful twist. "Do you need some berries, opichi?" She held out her red-stained palm. The bird pecked a berry, then another and another.

Mino prodded her with a paw. "All right, we'll all have our lunch together," Tanis laughed. Settling herself on a log, she took her piece of rice bread from her pocket. This was all she had. It had been the worst summer anyone could remember. The rain had drowned the garden plants. The fish had flickered away from the nets. The deer hid among the trees. Everyone in the village was hungry, their cheeks hollow, their ribs sharp.

Tanis ripped the bread into three. One piece was smaller than the others. Mino and Zaagi watched closely. She gave her dogs the bigger portions, keeping the littlest piece for herself. She swallowed it in two bites.

The opichi made a high twitter of alarm. Mino leaped to his feet, his fur bristling.

"What is it? What's wrong?" she gasped.

And then she smelled it—a stink of rotting fish and dirty flesh. She swallowed hard.

The opichi darted away. Mino barked wildly, leaping back and forward in terror. An icy wind blasted her face, the chill burrowing into her teeth and bones. Zaagi seized her skirt in his mouth and tugged her to her feet.

Something was coming. Something was coming through the forest, breaking the branches as it pushed past. The stink was growing stronger.

"Run!" she yelled. They sprinted between the trees, the snow flying beneath their feet. As the village came into view, Tanis saw a knot of people among the wigwams.

"Something's coming!" she shouted.

Everyone turned to her, their faces white with fear. "The windigo!" cried Binesi, one of the hunters. "Its claws!" He clasped his hands to his eyes. "It tried to snatch us ..."

Tanis had heard tales of the windigo. Grandma had told her how the windigo came in times of famine. It was filled with terrible hunger. But the more it ate, the hungrier it grew. Nothing could satisfy its belly, not deer, not elk, not hunters, not children ...

"What ... What shall we do?" Tanis gasped.

"There's nothing we can do," groaned Okwi. "When the windigo comes, all is lost. We must flee. We stand the best chance if we go our separate ways!"

"No, no," Tanis moaned. "Grandma will know what to do." She ran toward Grandma's wigwam, at the edge of the village under the pines.

"Grandma!" she cried, ducking into the warm darkness of the wigwam.

Grandma was crouching on the skins, whittling a stick of sumac with her knife. "So it's come," said the old woman. "I knew it would. I heard that, over in the village beyond the lake, they are so hungry that one of the hunters stole from his friends. Mitig, he's called." She spat into the fire. "In the winter, when we turn on each other, each one for themself, that is when the windigo comes."

"There must be something we can do," Tanis despaired. Tears pricked her eyes.

Grandma looked up, her face marked by long years of work and worry. "The windigo is stronger than any hunter, hungrier than any wolf. There is no pity in its heart of ice, no gentleness in its jagged claws. Would you want to fight such a creature?"

Tanis gulped.

"Yes ... I mean ... Yes, I want to save the village."

Grandma nodded, her eyes glinting. She gave her granddaughter the two sticks of sumac she had been peeling. They were as long as the girl's arms. "Take these sticks, little one. Go and fight the windigo."

"With sumac sticks?" gasped Tanis.

"Don't forget that small things can be powerful," answered Grandma.

Without looking back, the girl strode through the village, clasping the sticks tightly in her fists. Zaagi and Mino trotted close by her side. The villagers watched them pass.

Tanis and her dogs strode into the forest, the stench of rot growing stronger as they walked deeper into the shadows. It grew colder and colder. The branches crackled with frost. The girl's heart fluttered in her chest like a bird trying to break free and fly away to safety.

Zaagi whimpered. Something shifted in the darkness and Tanis cried out in fear. The windigo crawled from its hiding place, huge and stinking. It was like nothing she'd ever seen before. It crouched, spider-like, its long, folded limbs waiting to spring. Its skin was both as dark as the darkest midnight and as bright as the lights that sometimes danced in the sky. Powerful muscles rippled across its body, but its head was no more than a skull, with all flesh long since gone, and it had great long horns that curled among the branches. The girl shivered in the monster's deadly cold.

With a sickening snarl, a black dog darted from the gloom. Its lip curled, showing its vicious teeth. The beast was four times the size of poor Mino and Zaagi. Like any hunter, the windigo had a dog to snatch its kill.

Mino and Zaagi shrank back among Tanis's skirts. She felt them shaking with fear and cold. Then, with a brave bark, both Mino and Zaagi darted at the windigo's evil dog. Startled, the black beast turned and scampered through the trees, chased by Mino and Zaagi.

Tanis was alone with the windigo. The squatting monster towered above her, as tall as a tree, as wide as a torrent. The windigo flicked out a long tongue. Taking its slow time, it licked its hungry lips. It was picking its moment to pounce.

Her arms shaking, Tanis lifted her sticks. The windigo stared at her, its eye sockets unblinking. What could she do with sticks? If she tried to hit the creature, it would swat her away like a fly. She wanted to run, she wanted to be home in her warm wigwam. But she gripped her sticks tighter. The windigo lunged, opening its mouth wide—

Out of the corner of her eye, she glimpsed a flash of red feathers. The little opichi darted between her and the windigo. The windigo turned its head. Tanis hurled the sticks as hard as she could.

As Grandma's sumac sticks swung through the air, they turned from dull wood into shining copper. The metal rods struck the windigo with a sonorous clang, like a knife on a frozen lake—and the windigo shattered. Its withered flesh smashed into a thousand shards of ice.

And there, where the windigo had been, crouched a man. He moaned as if startled from sleep.

"It's Mitig!" came an angry voice from behind her. "It's that hunter from beyond the lake. The one who stole food from his friends."

The villagers were coming out of the shadows. Someone put an arm round Tanis. Another clapped her on the back. Her heart was pounding.

Mitig looked confusedly around him. "I'm so hungry ..." he murmured.

"The windigo's a warning, a warning to all of us," said Grandma, pushing her way through the crowd. "The windigo comes when we give way to our selfish hearts. Only a truly generous heart can destroy it." She grabbed Mitig's jacket and hauled him to his feet. "We'll let your village elders deal with you."

The villagers murmured their agreement.

Zaagi and Mino trotted out of the bushes, their tails wagging. The girl knelt to hug them, letting them lick her face with their warm tongues. Grandma rested her hand on Tanis's tired head. "Because you helped that opichi, it helped you in return. Truly generous hearts recognize one another, little one."

Perching on a sumac branch, the opichi twittered happily.

Oochigeas
and the Invisible One

Based on Mi'kmaq myths

Beside a wide lake, among the marshes, was a village where the Mi'kmaq people had made camp for many generations. In a wigwam of maple poles and birch bark, lived a father and his three daughters.

The two oldest daughters were named Luntook and Kobet. They were tall and beautiful, with long, shining black hair. Their clothes were stitched from the finest skins. The youngest daughter was small and often ill. Her mother had died a few days after the girl was born. When she was a baby, while her older sisters were playing and her father was hunting, she had rolled onto the hot stones around the fire, burning her face. Since that day, whenever people looked at the girl, they saw only her burn. Everyone in the village called her Oochigeas, which means "burned-skinned girl."

Oochigeas's sisters never stopped teasing about her burned face. They pulled Oochigeas's hair so hard that it stuck out in tufts, like the feathers of a baby bird. They made Oochigeas do the hardest, dirtiest work. It was she who swept out the cinders and hung stinking, slippery fish to dry in the sun. Her clothes were ripped and stained.

At night, in the deep darkness of the wigwam, Oochigeas cried herself to sleep. Oochigeas knew that people are often teased for looking different. She knew that bullies hurt someone else so they can feel better about themselves. She told herself that the only imperfections worth caring about are the ones hidden on the inside. Her beautiful sisters looked perfect in every way, but Oochigeas saw their hearts. She told herself to have courage, to bear their unkindness bravely, but the tears still came. She bit her lip to stop her sobs from waking them.

One morning, as Oochigeas mended her father's moccasins, she heard Luntook and Kobet chatting excitedly. They were talking about a brother and sister who had set up their lodge in the village. The brother was said to be a mighty hunter and the strongest, bravest, most handsome man that anyone could imagine. Most extraordinary of all, he was invisible. The hunter's sister had announced that, if any girl in the village could see the Invisible One, he would marry her. Oochigeas wasn't sure that she ever wanted to get married, but she was definitely fascinated by the idea of an invisible man. And even if she never got to meet the fearless hunter himself, his sister sounded like she was interesting, too.

"Yesterday evening," gossiped Luntook, "I heard that Kitpu, Sisip, and Tia'm went down to the water's edge when the Invisible One was returning from hunting. They pretended they could see him. But the sister didn't believe a word they said. She sent them home with their tails between their legs!"

"That Sisip!" said Kobet, pulling a face. "She thinks she's so pretty, but she's nothing special. Why would the Invisible One let himself be seen by her? He'll only show himself to someone truly beautiful." She ran her fingers through her shining hair.

"We should go!" gasped Luntook. "We're prettier than all of them put together. Let's go down to the lake this evening. Everyone will be so jealous when he appears for us when he hasn't appeared for them!"

"Can I come?" asked Oochigeas.

"Shut up, ugly," snapped Kobet. "How could you see the Invisible One?"

"No, no, I didn't mean …" Oochigeas trailed off as her sisters laughed.

That evening, as the sun started to dip toward the lake, Luntook and Kobet bustled down to the water's edge. They were dressed in their finest smocks and wearing strings of shells and beads around their necks.

The Invisible One's sister was waiting for her brother. She greeted the sisters kindly. "Here my brother comes now," she said. "Can you see him?"

Kobet frowned. All she could see was the rippling water, reflecting nothing but trees and birds. She looked at her sister. Luntook shrugged.

Kobet was certain that she would make a perfect wife for the Invisible One, unlike all the other plain and dull village girls. She would not be defeated by the small fact of not being able to see him. "I can see him!" she lied. "He's so handsome!"

Luntook narrowed her eyes at her sister. "Me too!" she yelled, pointing at the air over the muddy bank.

The Invisible One's sister nodded. "What is his bowstring made of?" she asked.

Luntook knew that bowstrings are always made out of sinew. "Deer sinew, of course," she answered.

The Invisible One's sister nodded. "What is his cloak made of?" she asked.

"The finest moose skin," answered Kobet quickly.

The Invisible One's sister sighed. "You cannot see my brother, but I wish you well. Good night."

Spluttering with rage and humiliation, Luntook and Kobet stamped back to their wigwam. Oochigeas listened to their bitter complaints as she served their food. While she washed the

pots, she wondered if maybe she could take a try at seeing the Invisible One. She knew, of course, that she would never be able to see him. It was just that she wanted a chance to try, like all the other village girls. She wanted to tell herself, even if no one else cared, that she was worth more than cinders and fish bones.

The next evening, as the sun began to sink, Oochigeas decided to set out. She looked down at her bare, dirty feet. She plucked at her ripped dress. She ran her fingers through her uncombed hair. She touched her face. There was no magic that would change the way she looked. She was as she was.

Trying to hold her head high, Oochigeas walked past her sisters.

"Where do you think you're going?" shouted Kobet.

"To the lake," murmured Oochigeas.

"Hah!" yelped Luntook. "The little idiot thinks she can see the Invisible One. With a face like that!"

Oochigeas's sisters chased after her, laughing so hard they had to hold their sides. "Hey, Sisip," they hooted. "Oochigeas thinks she'll be able to see the Invisible One."

Sisip laughed. Oochigeas tried not to hear the laughter, tried not to see the villagers coming out of their wigwams as she walked past.

When Oochigeas got to the lake shore, her eyes were so blurred with tears that she could hardly see the Invisible One's sister. The girl came to stand beside Oochigeas and said gently, "Here my brother comes now. Can you see him?"

Oochigeas rubbed the tears from her eyes. She was too embarrassed to speak, but she managed to smile at the Invisible One's sister.

"Look," said the sister. "Can you see him?"

Oochigeas looked toward the lake. A hunter was pulling his canoe up the muddy bank. He raised his hand in greeting. Oochigeas gulped. He turned toward her, holding his bow and looking very handsome indeed.

"What is his bowstring made of?" asked the Invisible One's sister.

"Oh," gasped Oochigeas. The hunter's bowstring glowed red, orange, green, and blue, as when the sun shines through rain. "It's a rainbow!" Oochigeas managed to say.

"What is his cloak made of?" asked the Invisible One's sister.

The hunter's cloak rippled behind him, the light of a trillion stars glimmering and twinkling in its midnight folds. Oochigeas clasped her hand to her mouth. "It's the road of the spirits, the Milky Way," she breathed.

Before Oochigeas knew what was happening, the Invisible One's sister was hugging her tightly. "Only a girl with a truly beautiful heart can see my brother," she said.

The Invisible One walked over, smiling broadly. "I am so glad to meet you!" His eyes were bright and friendly.

"Please come home with us," said the Invisible One's sister, taking Oochigeas by the hand. "There's dinner waiting for you."

Oochigeas soon found herself eating mouthfuls of steaming salty stew. While they all ate their fill, the brother and sister asked Oochigeas about her life and listened kindly to her answers.

When the Invisible One went outside to chop firewood, his sister persuaded Oochigeas to accept a smock of the softest moose skin. She stroked Oochigeas's blistered feet and eased them into beautifully embroidered moccasins. She combed Oochigeas's hair, patiently teasing out every single knot. She kissed Oochigeas's burned cheek.

"Please come and live with us," said the sister. "You and I can be sisters. I've always wanted a sister, more than anything in the world. You're even lovelier than I could ever have hoped. There's no need to marry my brother or anyone else, not unless you want to, when you're old enough to decide for yourself."

"I would love to live with you," said Oochigeas, her heart filled with joy. And so she did.

Pele Fights With Her Sister

Based on Hawai'ian myths

Long ago, soon after the gods had created the islands of Hawai'i, the wise goddess Haumea and her husband Kanaloa had two daughters. The first was Nāmaka, and very shortly after came Pele. The family lived on the island of Tahiti, many days' voyage from Hawai'i across the blue ocean. Both children had great gifts—when Nāmaka cried, her tears soaked her shawl, flooded the hut, then gathered into a stream that rushed to the ocean. When Pele laughed, she scattered showers of sparks, and when she clapped her hands, flames flickered around her fingers.

As Pele grew, she showed herself to be loving and clever, but she was quick to anger and slow to forgive. Everyone was drawn to Nāmaka's beauty and spirit, but when she was angry, her shouts grew into howling winds that whipped the ocean into foaming waves. And Nāmaka was often angry, usually with Pele.

Haumea knew that Pele and Nāmaka were the greatest goddesses ever born—the goddess of fire and the goddess of the ocean. Haumea was proud, but she was also afraid of what her fierce, stormy daughters would do.

One day, Pele and Nāmaka were sitting on the seashore. For once, Nāmaka was letting Pele braid her shining hair. Nāmaka was singing softly, a song of birds and waves. Pele's heart was calm. At times like this, she loved her sister and knew that her sister loved her. Suddenly, Nāmaka jerked her hair out of Pele's fingers.

"Who's that?" gasped Nāmaka, sending a flurry of blown sand over Pele's dress.

A boy was walking along the beach toward them. He was tall and quite handsome, Pele supposed. Nāmaka rushed over to greet the newcomer, leaving Pele all alone.

The boy was called Aukelenuiaiku. He and Nāmaka quickly struck up a friendship, and soon she was spending most of her time with him. She loved to make him laugh by sending clouds scudding across the sky. Nāmaka had no time for her sister now. Pele's heart burned with jealousy. Sparks flew whenever she tossed her head or stamped her foot. Haumea watched and sighed.

One evening, when Nāmaka and Aukelenuiaiku were walking along the shore, Pele called to her sister: "Mother needs you, Nāmaka!"

As soon as Nāmaka was gone, Pele put her plan into action.

"Are you cold, Aukelenuiaiku? It's getting dark," she asked the boy slyly.

"A little," said Aukelenuiaiku with a friendly smile.

"Watch this," boasted Pele. She rubbed her palms together until flames danced in her hands. With a flourish, Pele threw sparks into the air.

Aukelenuiaiku laughed, his eyes wide with wonder. Now he would have no time for Nāmaka's boring cloud tricks, thought Pele. She would have her sister back.

"What do you think you're playing at?" came Nāmaka's angry voice from behind Pele.

Pele turned. Her older sister was too clever by far. "Nāmaka, I ..."

Nāmaka took a deep breath, then blew. The gust pushed Pele off her feet and onto her back in the cold water. Now Pele was angry. She hurled a fistful of flame at her sister's head. Nāmaka ducked and, with a sweep of her arm, pulled the water into a great wave. It grew taller and taller, breaking over Pele and tumbling her head over heels, filling her nose and mouth with choking water ...

Strong arms pulled Pele to her feet. When she could open her stinging eyes, she saw it was her mother, Haumea. Aukelenuiaiku was running away down the beach, Nāmaka chasing after him.

"Pele, I have foreseen this," said Haumea calmly. "You must leave the island."

"No, Mother, please," cried Pele. "Make her leave, not me!"

"It must be you, Pele," said Haumea. "Take your father's canoe and follow the stars to the north."

Pele knew that Haumea's wisdom was as deep as the ocean. Blinded by tears, Pele let her mother lead her to the canoe and fill it with food and fresh water.

"I have a gift for you, my fierce daughter." Very gently, Haumea gave Pele a shining egg. "I am not sending you alone. Take care of this egg until it hatches. A little sister is growing inside. Be kind to her."

And so it was that Pele, holding the precious egg close to her chest, paddled away from Tahiti.

As night fell, Pele began to feel frightened. The ocean was wide, its waves dark and strong. The little canoe was tossed helplessly from side to side, despite the wooden float lashed to its side for balance. Pele's powers were no use to her here. She had never felt so alone, so far from home. Yet the egg was warm against her chest. Her heart warmed in answer.

Pele watched the stars prickle into life in the sky. She looked for the familiar shapes

she had learned to spot since she was young; the five stars of the Canoe-Bailer, the long twinkling line of the Backbone, and the Chief's Fishline. She turned to the north. All night she paddled, her arms aching with the endless effort.

When the sun rose on Pele's right, she let herself rest her head on the side of the canoe, just for a moment. She tucked the egg safely beside her. She slept.

Pele dreamed that Nāmaka was shouting at her. "I have lost Aukelenuiaikuuuuuuu .... I will never forgive yoooooooou ..." she howled. In Nāmaka's fury, she tossed Pele into the air like a broken twig.

Pele ripped open her eyes. Her dream was real! The sky was black, the rain falling like furious tears. The wind howled. The waves were tall as mountains, throwing the boat up, up, up—then pushing them down into the darkness. Nāmaka had blown up a terrible storm. She would drown Pele and the egg in her fury. Shivering with fear and cold, Pele curled around her egg. Her eyes shut tight, she shouted promises to the egg, anything to drown out Nāmaka's howls: "I will take care of you ... We will be best friends ..."

After what seemed like days, Nāmaka's cries quietened. The boat shuddered and was still. Pele opened her eyes. She gasped with relief. The sky was blue. The storm had driven the canoe onto the shore of an island. Green leaves and vivid flowers lined a beach of golden sand.

"I will call this island Niʻihau," said Pele to her egg, giving its shell a stroke. "Let's get warmed up."

Pele took a stick and dug a fire pit. Then she rubbed her hands until flames leaped into life. Smoke rose into the clear sky.

Now a crack appeared in the egg, growing and spreading until the shell crumbled. A little girl stepped out of the shards, her brown eyes bright. Pele kissed her.

"Aloha, little sister," said Pele kindly. "I'm so glad you're here. Can I call you Hiʻiaka?"

"Aloha, big sister," said the little girl, giving a wide smile.

Pele's heart grew hot with joy. She began to sing, about her gift of fire, about their journey, about her love for Hiʻiaka.

As Pele sang, Hiʻiaka started to dance. It was the very first hula that was ever danced.

Hi'iaka moved her arms like flames, like waves. She bent and twisted like the canoe. Pele could not help but join in.

Yet, as the sisters danced and laughed, Nāmaka was watching the smoke from Pele's firepit curl into the sky. Nāmaka wished the storm had drowned her deceitful sister. Her own anger had frightened away Aukelenuiaiku for ever. Nāmaka could not bear to think that Pele might be happy.

Nāmaka called on sharp-toothed Kāmohoali'i, god of sharks, to carry her to Ni'ihau. There, she stood in the shallows and watched Pele and Hi'iaka dance as if they had not a care in the world.

With a scream of fury, Nāmaka blew up a monstrous wave. She blew the wave up the beach, flooding Pele's firepit with saltwater and startled crabs. She blew the wave till she had thrown Pele and Hi'iaka into a tangle of arms and legs.

Coughing and spluttering, Pele and Hi'iaka scrambled for the canoe. Pele paddled as hard as she could for the nearest island, Kaua'i. There Pele dug a firepit to warm them.

Yet Nāmaka would not give up. Once more, she flooded Pele's firepit with icy waves. And so it happened again and again, on each of the islands in the Hawai'ian chain, until Pele and Hi'iaka landed on the southernmost, and biggest, island.

Gasping for breath, Pele climbed to the top of a tall mountain. There she dug a firepit deeper and wider than any she had dug before. She made a blaze so hot it melted the rock itself. The glowing rock flowed down the mountainside. Pele was proud. Her powers were no less fearful than her sister's.

Then, her arms folded, Pele waited for Nāmaka. Little Hi'iaka stood behind her fiery sister.

Nāmaka was soon splashing through the surf.

"So you want a fight, Nāmaka?" yelled Pele. "I'll give you one!" With all her strength, Pele hurled a fireball at Nāmaka, then another and another.

Nāmaka dodged and ducked, Pele's fireballs splashing sizzling water into the sky. Nāmaka huffed and howled, flooding the beach, her wind tearing up the trees from their roots. Pele spat furious flames, burning flowers, leaves, and grass. The lava from her firepit surged downhill, destroying everything in its path. Birds and bats rose into the air, squawking with fright.

"Pele, stop!" gasped Hi'iaka. "The animals ... You'll destroy the island!"

Now Pele saw the terrified animals, the burning forest. She clasped her hands to her mouth. She took a look at Nāmaka. Pele had never seen her sister look so sad.

Pele took a deep breath. "I'm sorry, Nāmaka, I just wanted you to want to play with me. I was jealous, and I took it way too far." she said.

Nāmaka wiped her eyes. "I'm sorry, too. I should have made time for my little sister." she sighed.

And so, as the flames died and the ocean drew back, the three sisters sat on the sand. Even today, you can find them there. Pele makes her home in the firepit of the great volcano of Kilauea. When the sisters are angry with each other, Kilauea spits burning rock at the stormy ocean. But when the sisters are happy, they dance a hula together on the sand.

Oshun Brings Water

Based on Yoruba myths

The Yoruba people of West Africa have always known that Olodumare was the father of creation. He created all of time and space. His children were called the Orisha. The first sixteen were male. There was Sango, who made thunder with his heavy axe. Fierce Ogun was the finest swordsman. Obatala had skilled, busy hands. Quick-thinking Orunmila was the wisest of them all.

The seventeenth and last Orisha was a little girl, named Oshun. Oshun was shy and quiet. She was not sure what she was good at. She worried about what her father Olodumare expected of her.

Olodumare called the seventeen Orisha to him. "I have a task for you. You must create land and people to live on it. You must work together. If you do not, you will fail." Then Olodumare went to sit far away.

The Orishas crowded together excitedly. Oshun was not as quick, or as tall, as her brothers. All she could see was their broad backs. All she could hear was mumbling.

Oshun tugged on Sango's robe to try to get his attention. She stood on tiptoe to try

to see over her brothers' shoulders. She tried to squeeze between the folds of their robes, but still none of them paid any attention to their little sister.

"I probably wouldn't be able to help anyway," thought Oshun miserably.

Then she went to sit where she sat whenever she felt left out—on the moon. She swung her legs in the empty sky. She nibbled at her nails. She twisted strands of hair between her anxious fingers.

Wise Orunmila soon came up with a plan. All the brothers agreed that Obatala should carry it out, since he was the best with his hands.

The brothers collected four things—an empty snail shell, a white chicken, a palm nut, and a long, gold chain.

Obatala filled the snail shell with sand, then placed it carefully inside his bag, along with the palm nut. He tucked the wriggling chicken under his arm. Then all the brothers laid their strong hands on one end of the gold chain. They threw out the other end of the chain so that it fell, jangling, through the swirling sky below them. The chain swung in the emptiness.

Fifteen of the brothers held tight to the chain, one behind the other, digging in their heels and bracing their bent knees. Obatala took a deep breath, grabbed hold of the chain, and swung his legs over the edge of the sky. He began to climb down the chain, squeezing tight to it with his fists and feet. Down and down he climbed, as his brothers gritted their teeth with the effort of holding him.

"Now?" called Obatala.

"A little lower," called back Orunmila.

Obatala shuffled lower. "Now?" he called.

"Now!" shouted Orunmila.

Letting go of the chain with one shaking hand while keeping a grip on the squawking chicken, Obatala felt around in his bag and pulled out the snail shell. Then he tipped the shell, trickling all the sand into the nothingness below him.

Hoping, willing, that Orunmila's plan had worked, Obatala let go of the chain— let himself fall. After a sickening moment of flailing arms and pounding heart, his feet

skidded in soft, warm sand. Sand stretched as far as he could see. He had created land.

Now Obatala placed the white chicken on the ground.

Delighted to be free, the chicken pecked curiously at the sand. Then it scratched at the ground with its claws, kicking up showers of sand behind its feathery back. The sand fell into heaps, some steep and others small. All day the chicken scratched and scattered the sand, creating all the world's mountains and valleys.

Now Obatala dug a hole in the ground and buried his palm nut. In a moment, no more than the blink of an Orisha's eye, the nut shell cracked and a shoot searched its way to the surface. The shoot grew into a tall tree. Ripening in the tree were pine nuts, which fell to the ground and sprouted into trees, which dropped more pine nuts.

Obatala's brothers were too far away to shout instructions. He knew he must carry out the most difficult portion of his task entirely alone. With his long fingers, he dug deep into the sand, down to where he felt thick, sticky clay. He squeezed and rolled the clay in his palms, examined his work, then pressed and pinched again. At last, he was pleased

with what he had made—a human. Now he created another and another, human after human. Each one looked a little different, but he was proud of every one of them.

From her perch on the moon, Oshun watched Obatala at work. She gripped the dusty rock, her knuckles white, as Obatala climbed heavily up the chain to his cheering brothers. Careful not to tumble, she leaned far forward to see the humans her brother had made. She clapped her hands with delight when she saw the people talking and laughing. Best of all were the little children, running this way and that as they played.

But, as Oshun watched, she saw something terrible happening. The humans fell silent. They crawled into the shade of the palms. The tall palms were browning and drooping. Cracks opened in the hard-baked ground.

"Water," murmured Oshun. "They need water."

The brothers had seen the problem too. Desperate to save their people, they called out to Olodumare: "Father, Father, please help us! Please give us water, Father!"

But Olodumare was sitting too far away to hear them.

"Oh!" gasped Oshun, her hands pressed to her mouth. She must do something before it was too late. She looked up at the sky, where a single cloud was sailing across the sun. Without asking herself if she was clever enough, or strong enough, or brave enough, Oshun transformed herself into a canary. Her yellow dress became yellow feathers, the shade of flower petals and ripe harvests.

Oshun fluttered into the sky, her wings beating fast. Her tiny beak fell open with the effort of battling the wind.

Oshun's brothers realized at once what their little sister was trying. "Oshun, be careful!" they shouted into the sky. "You'll hurt yourself! You're too little! Come back!"

But Oshun only thought of the poor, thirsty people below. Buffeted this way and that, she struggled higher and higher, closer to the cloud—and closer to the sun. The heat singed her feathers, but Oshun flew on. The feathers fell from her face and neck, but Oshun flew on. And as she flew, brave Oshun's wings grew wider and stronger. And now Oshun was a vulture, her wings brown, her face and neck bare of feathers, like every vulture that has ever lived.

At last, with the sun's flames licking at her wingtips, Oshun's hooked beak burst the cloud. Water drenched her feathers. And as Oshun swerved and turned, every beat of her wings sent a flurry of raindrops to the ground. The rain soaked the cracked mud. People cupped their hands and drank cool, sweet water.

Now Oshun knew what she was good at. She knew what her father Olodumare had expected of her.

When Oshun landed, her brothers gathered around her. They told her they were sorry they had forgotten Olodumare's words of warning. They told her they had learned that if they did not work together, they would fail.

"Even the littlest sister must be listened to," said Sango.

In the hills of Yorubaland, rainwater pooled and started to flow, forming a wide river that snaked to the sea. Slender-snouted crocodiles paddled through the water, snapping at tilapia and catfish. Along the banks waved reeds and grasses. Fruit trees, from star apples to butterfruit, sent roots into the moist soil. In gratitude to the Orisha, the people called the river Oshun, which means "flow."

To this day, in a sacred grove beside the river, people gather every year to praise Oshun. Wearing seashells, their faces painted with fish, people celebrate Oshun, the Orisha of water, the bringer of life, and the listener to those who are lost or lonely.

The Trials of Étaín

Based on Irish myths

Long ago, the gods and goddesses of Ireland walked the land. In those days, they did not hide themselves away beneath the ground. They were brave and powerful. Sometimes, they were vengeful and cruel. The gods and goddesses called themselves the Tuatha Dé Danann, the folk of the great mother goddess Danu.

The loveliest of all the goddesses was Étaín. Every morning, the sun waited for Étaín to wake before it would rise into the sky. When Étaín fell asleep, the tired sun let itself dip below the horizon. Étaín always wore a robe of flaming red. Her true love was the god Midir. He held power over Ireland's rivers, guiding them across the land to give water to the meadows and woods.

When Étaín and Midir married, they made their home in a fort at the top of a hill at the very heart of Ireland. A carpet of the greenest grasses and most beautiful wildflowers stretched in all directions, as far as the eye could see. Étaín and Midir looked forward to a life of love and laughter. All the Tuatha Dé Danann wished happiness on the bright newlyweds. All except one.

The sorceress Fúamnach had not been invited to the wedding feast. Fúamnach's powers were those of darkness and destruction. On her shoulder perched a clever raven as black as night. The bird left the witch's side only to flap over the battlefields, where it watched greedily for fallen warriors. Fúamnach could not bear the shining happiness of Étaín and Midir. She decided to end it.

Fúamnach galloped to Étaín and Midir's fort on her black stallion. She banged on the sturdy oak door, the noise echoing through the corridors like thunder.

Étaín greeted the sorceress bravely. It was forbidden for her to refuse to invite a visitor in, no matter who they were. The sweet goddess led the witch into the feasting hall and offered her a goblet of mead. Midir was away, hunting with his manservants.

"My lady Fúamnach," said Étaín with a curtsey. "I hope you can forgive me for not inviting you sooner. But please know you will always be welcome here—"

"Nonsense," hissed Fúamnach, her black eyes narrowing. Her raven gave a rasping cry.

Étaín drew back, clutching her red robe in her fist. "My lady, I hope we can be friends ..." she gasped.

Baring her sharp teeth, Fúamnach drew a wand of rowan from her cloak. Before Étaín had time to run or even think, the witch struck Étaín with the wood. And Étaín the goddess was gone. In her place was a pool of water.

Satisfied with the first part of her plan, Fúamnach set off in pursuit of Midir.

The horrified sun peered through the window at the pool of water. The water began to dry in the warmth. As the pool shrank, it formed into a small, red worm. The worm wriggled and stretched. It crawled across the boards. Then the worm curled into a brilliant scarlet fly. The fly tested its flimsy wings, then flew out of the window. For the fly was Étaín and she must find Midir before the witch cast her spell on him.

Étaín fluttered across the meadows and bogs. Her wings shimmered in the sunlight. Her eyes shone like rubies. The fluttering of Étaín's wings made a sound sweeter than the strings of a harp, clearer than the chiming of bells.

Fúamnach's keen ears heard this lovely sound. At once, the witch blew up a wind so wild that poor Étaín was dashed against rocks and hurled into tree trunks. Year after

year, the wind blew. Étaín had not a moment's rest. Every time she saw a flower where she might settle, every time she glimpsed a mossy bed where she might crawl, the wind blew her away with the dust and leaves.

Her wings bruised and torn, her heart aching, Étaín was eventually blown through a window and into the home of a man named Étar and

his wife Ness. Hurtling head over wings, Étaín landed in a goblet of wine. Ness lifted the goblet to her lips and swallowed the drink, Étaín and all.

And so it was that, 1,012 years after her first birth, Étaín was born again. The following spring, Ness had a baby girl so beautiful that the sun itself was put to shame. The couple had heard old stories of the Tuatha Dé Danann and the loveliest goddess of them all, Étaín. The couple called their daughter Étaín.

Ness and Étar loved Étaín; and Étaín loved them. Ness always dressed her pretty daughter in red. Although Étaín had no memory of who she had been, she often told her laughing mother that she was truly a fairy princess. She did not believe that gods had ever walked the land, but she begged to hear her mother's tales of fairies that crept from cracks in the ground. In her dreams, Étaín saw a sad boy called Midir, who seemed to call to her.

When Étaín was old enough to go out into the world alone, she took a long walk across the green grass and wildflowers that grew on a steep hill, at the very heart of Ireland. With a great gust, the wind blew leaves into Étaín's face—and suddenly she knew who she was. She knew that Midir was imprisoned here beneath the ground.

Étaín stamped her foot, the noise echoing like thunder through the corridors below. "Fúamnach," she bellowed, "let me in! You cannot refuse me. Just as I welcomed you into my home all those years ago, let me in!"

A crack opened between Étaín's feet. She crawled inside, into the darkness. Following a glimmer of light on the rocky walls, Étaín shuffled into a cavern. And there sat Fúamnach, her eyes as black and her raven as vicious as before.

"You've taken your time," said Fúamnach with a sharp-toothed grin.

"Let me have Midir," said Étaín.

"You think you can just walk in and ask for him?" cackled Fúamnach.

Étaín stood firm, her hands gripped into fists so tight that her nails pierced the skin.

"I'll make you an offer," said Fúamnach. "Every day, Midir and I play a game of fidchell." She pointed at the stone board and carved pieces that sat ready on a table, lit by streaks of sunlight from an opening in the rock above. "I told Midir that if he can beat

me, he can leave." She giggled. "He plays poorly. If you can beat me, you can have him."

Étaín remembered playing fidchell long, long ago. "I will hold you to your bargain," she said. She seated herself by the board, opposite the witch.

The fidchell board had seven squares along each side, making a grid of forty-nine. In the very middle of the board was the king made of solid gold. Surrounding the king were the silver pieces, his defenders. Guarding the edges of the board were the bronze pieces, the attackers.

"I shall play bronze, of course," said Fúamnach.

"Of course," said Étaín. If Étaín was playing silver, she must clear a path for the king to escape the board by surrounding and removing the bronze pieces. For her part, Fúamnach would try to capture the silver pieces by surrounding them with her own.

Fúamnach made the first move, pushing a bronze piece toward one of the silver pieces. Étaín had a choice—she could move her piece to the side to escape or she could respond by attacking a bronze piece, forcing Fúamnach to defend. She attacked. After three moves, Étaín had captured one of Fúamnach's pieces, but the witch had also taken one of the silvers. Fúamnach was a skilled player. Étaín gazed at the trapped king. She must focus, she must form a plan.

After nine moves, Fúamnach had captured three silver pieces, while Étaín had only two bronze pieces. Étaín's palms were sweating. How could she ever clear the king's path? Then she saw a weakness: Fúamnach had left one of her pieces isolated. If Étaín could capture that piece, she would have cleared a path. But it was vital that she distract Fúamnach from her plan. On the other side of the board, Étaín moved one of her silvers pieces into a risky position to attract the sorceress's attention. Fúamnach snatched the piece triumphantly.

"Aaah," sighed Étaín, "it seems you are a better player than I am. Will you grant me a wish before I lose? May I see Midir one last time?"

Delighted with the way the game was going, Fúamnach cackled. "One last glimpse of your husband for you. One last glimpse of the sunlight for him." With a wave of the sorceress's hand, Midir appeared in the cavern, blinking his eyes in the light.

"Étaín!" he cried, rushing to her side.

Étaín grasped Midir's hand, squeezing it tight. Her eyes filled with tears but she blinked them away. Now was not the time for weakness.

"My turn, I think," said Étaín. And with one move, she surrounded Fúamnach's lonely bronze piece and cleared the king's path.

Fúamnach shrieked, her raven flapping from her shoulder with a hideous squawk.

"I win," said Étaín. Drawing a deep breath, the goddess transformed herself and Midir into swans, their feathers white as snow.

The swans took to the air, flying through the hole in the rock and into the bright blue sky. Soaring above the heather, above the woods and rivers, they flew side by side toward the sun.

And from that day forward, the people of Ireland knew that true love would always win, just as the sun will always rise after the dark night.

Xquic and the Empty Net

Based on Maya myths

In the early days of the world, things like the weather and the seasons did not just happen on their own. The gods in charge of such things needed to be thanked and celebrated, so they would remember to send the rains on time, or the right amount of sunshine for all the plants to grow and the animals to thrive.

Two of these gods, Plumed Serpent, who lived in the ocean and Heart of Sky, who lived in the clouds, decided to try to make the first humans, so they would always have some people who remembered them. From the mud of what is now Mexico, they formed humans. But these first humans were not a success. As soon as they tried to walk and talk, they crumbled back into dirt.

Plumed Serpent and Heart of Sky went to ask the advice of two of the wisest gods, Grandfather Xpiacoc and Grandmother Xmucane. They were said to be able to predict the future. Xpiacoc and Xmucane scratched their heads, but said that humans might be able to be carved from wood.

The wooden humans soon spread across the earth, chattering loudly. Yet the creators saw there was nothing in the hearts of the wooden humans. They did not remember their makers and they did not care to consult the calendar. Heart of Sky sent rain both day and night. Most of the wooden humans were washed away by the great flood. Those that survived were set upon by their cooking pots and brooms.

Grandmother Xmucane knew what to do. She ground up white and yellow maize, then added a little water. Working carefully, she shaped people from the sticky paste.

The people lay motionless, no breaths lifting their chests, no thoughts flickering their eyelids. Yet Xmucane worked on and on. When her fingers were caked with paste, she washed them, saving the murky water in a bowl. As soon as Xmucane had made enough humans to people the world, she boiled the contents of her bowl. With a little spoon, she tipped a few drops of the broth into each human's mouth. Now the people breathed and thought and moved.

Everyone agreed the maize people were a success. They always remembered to praise their makers. They never forgot to count the calendar days so they could hold the proper festivals to make sure the sun still rolled across the sky, the moon still rose, and the stars still turned.

For many years, the maize people walked across the land, tracking wild animals and picking berries as they passed. At night, they slept close to their campfires, hoping to stay safe from jaguars and rattlesnakes. It was a hard life, always on the move, always looking over their shoulders, but the people knew nothing different.

Then one year, the sun passed too close to the land. The plants withered and the lakes dried. The animals crept away. Very soon, the people were hungry. They grew thin, thirsty, and frightened. Among them was a girl called Xquic.

Xquic could not bear to see her friends hungry. She determined to ask Grandmother Xmucane for help. The very next morning, Xquic pinched herself awake before dawn. She scrambled to the top of the highest hill. Shivering in the darkness, she waited for Chac Ek', the morning star, to rise.

At last, shining with a steady silvery light, Chac Ek' slipped over the horizon, leading the way for the sun itself.

"Grandmother!" cried Xquic in her loudest, bravest voice, her eyes fixed on Chac Ek'. "Please help us! We are starving. I don't know what to do!"

Xmucane's hearing was not as good as it used to be, but she heard the girl's sharp voice. Startled, she peered down at the girl on the hilltop. Xmucane's knees hurt. Her breath was short. She was certainly not in the habit of handing out help. But there was something about the girl, the way she gripped her hands into fists.

Xmucane's earrings shaking with the effort, her white hair flying, she appeared before the girl. Xquic gasped and fell to her knees.

"Get up, get up," snapped Xmucane. Into Xquic's quaking hands she thrust a net bag, quite empty. "Fill this bag with food."

"But how should I ... ?" murmured Xquic, putting her fingers through the empty net. When she looked up, Xmucane was gone.

In the orange light of the rising sun, Xquic walked down into the valley, looking everywhere for food to put in the bag. But the trees were empty. The birds had flown. She wondered if perhaps the bag was magic. She scooped handfuls of earth and pebbles into the bag. But they only slipped through the net.

Then Xquic saw a plant growing from a crack in the dusty ground. The plant did not seem very special. It had long, slim leaves and a tall stem crowned with reddish tufts. But peering closer, Xquic saw that, tightly wrapped in leaves, the plant bore a strange-looking fruit covered in rows of yellow teeth. She plucked one of the teeth between her nails, put it in her mouth, and bit. It burst sweetly on her tongue. Excited now, Xquic put the yellow fruit in her bag.

Yet the bag was still almost empty. Xquic had no idea how to turn the little teeth into enough food to fill the bag. She stamped her foot in frustration. She could not go back to her friends with nothing. She felt sobs rising, squeezing her throat and shaking her shoulders. "Oh, help me, help me, help me!" she cried.

A gentle hand touched Xquic's arm, the fingertips soft as a butterfly's wings.

"I am Ixcanil, goddess of seeds," said a quiet voice.

Xquic swung around, her hand clutched to her fluttering heart. There stood a goddess, as bright as ripe fruit, as beautiful as an opening flower.

Now Xquic heard trickling water, the sound of a stream bubbling over mossy rocks.

"I am Ixtoj, goddess of rain," said a clear voice.

And standing before Xquic was a second goddess, her dress of rippling blue, her silken skin glistening with raindrops.

Now Xquic smelled a scent more delicious than any she had ever known, so rich and ripe that her mouth began to water.

"I am Ixcacao, goddess of chocolate," said a laughing voice.

And here was a third goddess, her brown eyes warm and her smile offering comfort and kindness.

Xquic did not know whether to cry or laugh, shout for joy or fall to her knees.

"Give me your ear of maize," said Ixcanil, taking Xquic's bag. She pulled out the yellow-toothed fruit. "Watch," she said, as she scraped furrows in the soil with her toe. Gripping the ear of maize with both hands, she twisted until the teeth popped off. They tumbled into the waiting furrows. "These yellow kernels are good to eat, but they can also be planted. Always save some to sow."

"The kernels must be watered," trilled Ixtoj, "or they will not grow." She tipped a clay jar, pouring water over the eager ground. At once, green shoots broke through the soil and, reaching for the sun, grew into tall stalks topped with red plumes.

"Listen," said Ixcacao with a chuckle, "these plumes are thick with pollen, even if it is too tiny for us to see." She wiggled a plume with her finger. "The wind must carry the pollen to other plants, so kernels can grow on every ear. Wait patiently until the kernels are ripe before you pick them. Then grind the kernels into flour or put them in a pan over the fire—then listen to them pop!"

Ixcacao laughed merrily, and held out a cup to Xquic. "Drink my chocolate," she said.

The cup was filled with a thick, brown, cold liquid. It was so long since Xquic had drunk or eaten anything. She sipped. The drink was bitter but delicious. As Xquic gulped, her heart filled with happiness. Xquic licked her sticky lips.

When Xquic looked up, the goddesses were gone. But, as far as she could see, the valley was covered by waving, golden maize. Every ear was ready to be picked.

Singing with joy, Xquic filled her net with ears of maize until it was too heavy to lift. Then she ran to fetch her friends. Amazed but beaming, they helped her harvest.

Xquic boiled her share of the maize kernels in lime water, then ground them into flour using a stone. She added a little water to make dough. Rolling and slapping the dough between her palms, she formed small, flat cakes. As she grilled the cakes over the fire, she decided to call them tortillas. Sometimes, when she was cooking for her friends, Xquic mixed her tortilla flour with chocolate and spiced it with chili.

And this was how, long ago, people in a valley in Mexico became the first to sow and harvest maize. These people no longer followed the wanderings of wild animals, but settled down to be farmers. Over the centuries, their villages grew into great cities, where they built stone pyramids to thank the gods and goddesses for their help. Their cities were the wonder of the world.